COPING WITH DIVORCE

COPING WITH DIVORCE

ROBERT A. RAAB

THE ROSEN PUBLISHING GROUP INC.

NEW YORK

Published in 1979, 1984 by The Rosen Publishing Group Inc.
29 East 21st Street, New York, N.Y. 10010

Copyright 1979 by Robert A. Raab

Revised Edition 1984

Library of Congress Cataloging in Publication Data

Raab, Robert.
  Coping with divorce.

  1. Divorce—United States. 2. Marriage—United
States. I. Title.
HQ834.R3   301.42'84   78-27751
ISBN 0-8239-0428-8

Manufactured in the United States of America

To my parents, Sam and Emma Raab, who lived through the agony of my late sister Joan's divorce and the tragic aftermath of it.

To all those who already have or soon may cope with divorce, may this book give some insight and help.

To the lonely, who—hopefully—will find the courage and wisdom to rebuild their lives after breaking up.

To the optimist in each of us who calls forth comfort and hope, despite the travail of the moment.

To the faint of heart who must find the inner strength to face each new day, and who do confront life with quiet dignity and courage.

> "I will walk within my house in the integrity of my heart." Psalm 101.2.

About the Author

DR. ROBERT A. RAAB is the Rabbi of the Suburban Temple, Wantagh, New York. He is Adjunct Professor of Sociology Department of Nassau Community College, Garden City, New York.

A native of Cleveland, Ohio, he received a B.A. degree from the University of Cincinnati and was ordained at the Hebrew Union College–Jewish Institute of Religion, where he earned the degree of Doctor of Hebrew letters. His alma mater also awarded him the honorary degree of Doctor of Divinity. He was graduated from the two-year Pastoral Counseling program of the Post-Graduate Center for Mental Health, in New

PHOTO BY MICHAEL ROSS

York City. He received an M.S.W. from Yeshiva University in 1981.

Before going to Wantagh, Dr. Raab was the Assistant Rabbi at Temple Sholom, Chicago, and Rabbi of Temple B'nai Israel, McKeesport, Pennsylvania. He was also a military chaplain in the United States Air Force during the Korean war.

Dr. Raab is the author of *The Teenager and the New Morality* and *Coping with Death*. He has also written articles for a number of religious and secular publications. He is past President of the Wantagh Clergy Council and of the Long Island Association of Reform Rabbis.

His wife, Dr. Marjorie Klein Raab, is an Administrator at Nassau Community College, where she does in-college research. They have two sons, Daniel, an attorney in Florida, and Joel, the program director of radio station WHN in New York.

Acknowledgments

In previous books I have acknowledged the special help given to me by Ruth Rosen, as well as the inspiration and encouragement I have received from my family—my dear wife Margie, my sons Daniel and Joel, and my wonderful parents, Sam and Emma. All of the aforementioned continue to be supportive in every way.

But this time I especially acknowledge my congregation, the Suburban Temple in Wantagh. This congregation and its leadership have always been supportive in everything I have undertaken. How lucky I am to be the Rabbi of such a fine group of people!

Preface

Divorce is a fact of life. Some might even say it is a fact of marriage. The rising divorce rate has produced figures indicating that at any given moment in America, at a minimum, some 12 million persons are involved in a divorce situation. In 1974 it was estimated that 3 million were divorced and 2 million were separated, with over 7 million children as products of these broken homes. This does not take into account those who are separated nor the unreported divorces (since not all states yield statistics on this matter).

With the rise of divorce and remarriage and then divorce again, it is important to look into the entire matter of how this problem affects the family.

Sociologists say that eight of every ten adults in America will be married at least once. Of those who divorce, the chances are strong that they will remarry. The barrier to divorce at one time was children. Today, in a self-oriented society where personal concerns and desires are paramount, the idea of holding an "empty-shell" marriage together for the sake of the children no longer has validity. Divorce is real and ever-present. It is no respecter of persons. The rich, the middle-class, and the poor experience it. Psychologists speak of the disfunctional aspects of modern life. Many couples are "out of sync" with each other.

This book will explore some of the facets of divorce in modern-day America. Divorce has become so common that it no longer excites adverse comment. Coping with divorce may be something very real in your life. The way you confront it can be the measure of maturity and insight.

Contents

COPING WITH DIVORCE

CHAPTER I

History and Statistics

Almost all societies provide for divorce. Anthropologists have noted that over half of all societies have divorce rates higher than those of the United States. "In some societies divorce is rare; while in others, a permanent union is unusual. Observers have reported that only about one Navajo in four lives with the same spouse all his life, and men commonly have several wives in succession. It is reported that in one Eskimo group, women sometimes marry and divorce several times in a single year. In most societies, public opinion tends to be opposed to divorce, but in a few societies social pressure serves to undermine the marital relationship. According to the American anthropologist George P. Murdock, Crow Indian men subject themselves to ridicule by living with the same woman too long. The general public view of most groups has been that divorce is unfortunate, but often necessary." [1] So, we see that our Western disapproval of divorce is not shared by all cultures.

There are records of early civilizations in which marriage was a social arrangement and the state had no input or authority. In such a situation, families could control marriage and divorce.

The Judaic Approach

In the Jewish tradition the Bible gives clear evidence of where authority is to be found: "Thy desire shall be to thy husband, and he shall rule over thee." The husband had control, even as the wife brought a dowry into the marriage. Theoretically divorce was easy. Even for the minor offense of "spoiling the soup" a man could sue for divorce. But a wife could also seek divorce if her husband was in an occupation that caused his body to smell unpleasantly; for instance, if he were a tanner of animal hides. Although divorce was theoretically easy, it was necessary for the husband to forfeit a specified amount of money if he sought to leave his wife. Since most people were poor, few were divorced. The religious divorce was called the "get," sometimes known as the "bill of divorcement."

---

[1] *Encyclopedia Americana*, Vol. 9.

It was given to the woman by the husband in the presence of a rabbinical court, which was convened to try to salvage the marriage. The Jews also had Leverite marriage, in which a man was compelled, if he were single, to marry his widowed sister-in-law. Refusal to do so meant a ceremony of public disgrace for the brother. In ancient times the father of the household had absolute power, although the Bible was one of the first religious documents to give women the right of inheritance. The duties of the Jewish woman were clearly defined: She was to be a wife and mother. However, Proverbs speaks of the woman who kept the business accounts of her husband and ran his business affairs while he sat and chatted with the men in the gates of the city.

Athens and Rome

Athenian law held that either spouse could seek and obtain divorce. Yet, as in Jewish biblical law, the Athenian male was favored and found it easier than the female to seek a separation. He could dismiss his wife for almost any cause that he saw fit to present. The wife could sue for divorce on the grounds of cruelty or degenerate behavior. She was not free just to leave her husband. He, however, was free to dismiss her on whatever grounds he presented. A modern feature of ancient Greek law was that divorce could be obtained by mutual consent. Today, we have "no-fault" divorce, which in some ways resembles the Athenian system. The one unusual twist was that in Greek law the children were always given to the father, rather than to the mother, when marriages were dissolved. Because most women were loath to give up their children, many endured very unhappy marriages.

Although early Roman law gave most of the power in divorce to the males, by 200 B.C. women were allowed to divorce their husbands at will. Men of the upper classes had great freedom to set aside their wives. Those of the highest ranks were polygamous. "The Roman statesmen Sulla and Pompey were each married five times. The method of divorce was simple. The man simply presented his wife with a letter declaring their mutual freedom. During the reign of Augustus Caesar (30 B.C. to 14 A.D.), laws were passed restricting divorce. The most important of these were the Julian laws conceived by Augustus in his old age to reform the morals of the Romans. The Julian laws brought marriage and divorce under the regulation of the state for the first time in Roman history." [2]

---

[2] Ibid.

Christian Tradition

Paul set the style for the early Christian faith. His practice was to forbid remarriage unless one of those in the original marriage was unconverted to Christianity. In the 6th century the code of Justinian sought to impose harsh male control over women. These stringent church laws were opposed by women and were soon modified. Even 1,500 years ago, women were asserting their rights in the Western world.

Christian canon law evolved to the point where separation could be granted on the basis of adultery, extreme cruelty, or withdrawal from the church by one of the partners to the union. "An annulment was the only method of securing complete freedom from one's spouse and the privilege of remarrying. . . . Over the years the canonical impediments came to be interpreted so broadly that some grounds could nearly always be found to terminate successfully the marriage of a person who possessed enough political power or influence." [3] Today, Catholics practice annulment, and in some dioceses this can be obtained with shortened waiting periods.

The Protestant Way

One of the reforms of Martin Luther was to make divorce a civil rather than a religious matter. Marriage was to lose its sacramental nature, and the state assumed control. The civil judge rather than the religious court was to become decisive. As the Reformation took hold, secular courts began to hear cases of adultery, cruelty, and desertion, and the king was given the power to decree a divorce. The film *A Man for All Seasons* depicts the struggle between King Henry and Sir Thomas More over whether or not Rome could decide whether a monarch could obtain a divorce. "In England between the years 1669 and 1850, only 229 divorces were granted, all but three or four of which were to men. Only in the mid-20th century did British divorce laws undergo further liberalization." [4]

Divorce Laws in the United States

The early colonies reflected, in their divorce laws, the practices of the countries of origin. Much of English common law was eventually incorporated into the American system. However, the United

---

[3] Ibid.
[4] Ibid.

States Constitution left marriage and divorce legislation up to the individual states, so the state legislatures were free to make the civil laws that were to govern marriage and divorce. For this reason, divorce laws vary from state to state. Unless one follows the no-fault pattern, the general approach in American courts is that one party must be guilty in a divorce proceeding. This can be traced to earlier ecclesiastical courts. The motive for divorce and the legal grounds for it are not always the same. Before New York State law was liberalized, adultery-by-arrangement was practiced, with the full knowledge and consent of the parties involved.

In Florida it is possible to be awarded rehabilitative alimony so that a spouse can become educated so as to obtain employment. For example, a wife works so that her husband can complete his college education, whereupon he seeks to divorce her. At that point she can ask for rehabilitative alimony so that she can go to school to get a degree. Since she supported him while he was in college, he now must support her so that she can get the college training that will lead to a job, making her self-supporting. Rehabilitative alimony can replace long-term or permanent alimony.

The law of divorce and alimony has become increasingly complicated. A wealthy client can find many loopholes in it to delay almost indefinitely the payments that he agreed to make to his former wife. And, for the first time, in some cases a wife is compelled to pay alimony to her husband; for example, where the wife is the breadwinner, and the man is a househusband who raises the children. Such cases are still far from common, however.

Statistics

The following figures on the median duration of U.S. marriages have been provided by the U.S. Public Health Service. The reporting states gave a median figure of 5.3 years in 1950, 7.1 years in 1960, 6.7 years in 1970, and 6.5 years in 1974. Thus, the results are uneven. What is distressing is that the average marriage in America has a life expectancy of less than eight years. At the same time, the number of divorces is on the increase. In 1910 there were 10.3 marriages and 0.9 divorces per 1,000 people. In 1950 it was 11.1 marriages and 2.6 divorces per 1,000 people. In 1970, we find 10.6 marriages and 3.7 divorces per 1,000 people. The latest available figures show that in 1980 there were 10.6 marriages and 5.0 divorces per 1,000 people. Thus, slightly less than twice as many people are getting married each year as are getting divorced. In

1981, 2,438,000 marriages were performed, and 1,219,000 divorces were granted. So, in 1981 there were 500 divorces for every 1,000 marriages, up slightly from 1980 when there were 490 divorces for every 1,000 marriages. Also 68.8 percent of females remarry after divorce while 78 percent of males find a new spouse.

How to Secure a Divorce

Divorce is largely a legal matter. Once the parties have decided to seek divorce, they go to an attorney. Books have been written on how to get a divorce by acting as your own attorney, but few avail themselves of this option.

In some cases, the couple first goes for marriage counseling. If this fails, they must turn to the courts. It is estimated that over half of all divorces are uncontested and settled out of court. The parties agree ahead of time to the terms of settlement. Where this is not possible, the divorce is contested. It should be noted that even in states having "no-fault" divorce (meaning that neither party is at fault), this can only be implemented if both parties agree to the concept. If one party feels slighted, no-fault is not possible. In some cases, the party that feels aggrieved may agree to no-fault after winning a pre-court monetary settlement. No-fault in the purest sense is not to be found. Sociologists and psychologists may say that the "situation" rather than the person is to blame, but the law usually seeks to place the blame on one or the other spouse in a contested divorce. The word "contested" means that there is an adversary relationship. The spouses are not in agreement. Each seeks to get the best monetary terms. Contested divorces can be bitter, protracted struggles that leave both spouses emotionally and financially drained.

The securing of a divorce is governed by the laws of the various states. In almost all states grounds for divorce include adultery, desertion, habitual drunkenness, imprisonment for commission of a felony, and incurable insanity. Sexual impotency is recognized as grounds for annulment in most states. Drug abuse and nonsupport are other factors widely accepted as a basis for divorce. Sometimes the parties agree to a legal separation before finalizing the divorce. This period can vary depending on state law. During the period of separation, the couple live apart while the terms of the divorce are worked out. If one spouse resists the divorce, the final decree can be endlessly delayed. This leads to bitterness and arguments. Often important financial matters must be settled. Who shall have the car, home, stocks, and other possessions? The lawyers try to get the best settlement for the party they represent. Bitterness is inflamed as the spouses see that they are, in truth, in a battle. The conflict can also extend to custody of the children, child support, and alimony. As more women enter the labor market, alimony figures drop.

In America, divorce is secured through secular legal means. For some people, such as Orthodox and Conservative Jews and Catholics, religious laws also must be followed, but religious divorces cannot stand alone. You may receive a religious divorce from your rabbi or an annulment from the priest, but the civil divorce is paramount. Without it, severe legal problems arise having to do with inheritance, rights of the spouses to remarry, and the like. Since the U.S. gives the civil courts jurisdiction, the religious courts lack the power to grant a divorce unless there has been a state-issued civil divorce. When you wed, a clergyperson acts as an officer of the state in performing the ceremony. When you divorce, it is the state and its laws that dissolve the relationship. America, then, follows the lead of the Reformation, which cast aside Catholic Church law and gave the power of divorce to the state.

In countries where religion is powerful, the law can be influenced by religion. In Israel today, religion has a powerful voice in determining whether or not a marriage shall take place, and religious groups have control in the matter of divorce as well. For example, it is the Orthodox Rabbinate that sets the rules for marriage and divorce. Reformers in Israel have a difficult time. Those who have demanded that church and state be separated in the matter of marriage and divorce laws have not yet won the day.

Figures Are Deceptive

It is popular to say that over 40 percent of all marriages end in divorce; however, figures must be interpreted. It is true that in a given year, say 1972, in the U.S. 2,269,000 marriages were recorded, and 839,000 divorces. Thus some might say that 37 percent of all marriages are ending in divorce. This is a false figure, since we are dealing only with the numbers of divorces and marriages recorded in a single year. We must remember that most marriages in a given year remain intact. Then, too, the population eligible to divorce is greater than the population eligible to marry, based on the accepted fact that most who marry in a given year are in the 18 to 28 age group. What can be said is that in a period of 40 years a given marriage has a 2 percent or 3 percent chance of dissolving in each year of the projected life span of the marriage. Most research indicates that the greatest number of divorces occur in the first three years of marriage. Although childless marriages seem to have the highest rate of divorce, the split-ups with children are increasing at a tremendous rate. Religious groups are reluctant to provide figures on divorce, so it is difficult even to guess what the religious breakdown might be. Some estimates indicate that Protestants have the highest divorce rate, followed by Catholics and Jews.

On a more optimistic note, it has been shown that approximately one-fourth of those who divorce are remarried within the year, and 75 percent are married again within nine years of divorce. A 1972 study showed that nine out of ten people marry at least once in their lives, usually at an early age. In 1980 the median age for marriage among women was around 22.1, and males wed at age 24.6.

Effect on Children

It is estimated that in 60 percent of current divorces, minor children are involved. "In 1935, there were only 68 children involved in every 100 divorces. By 1948, there were 74, and by 1957, there were 100s. Today, over one million children see their parents divorced each year."[5] If this figure continues on a yearly basis, there will be a continuing disruption of family life. On the brighter side, some researchers have said that the fact that more and more children are involved in divorce will make it somewhat easier. No longer will a child be the only one in the class who lacks a father and mother in the home. Some communities report that the majority of children in the primary grades are not living with two natural parents. Statistics show that over half of the children who come from unhappy homes reacted by feeling that divorce was the best way out of a difficult situation. But the majority of children who came from homes that they felt to be happy were shocked and disturbed by divorce and were against it. "Almost half of these youngsters (44 percent) reported that they felt 'used' by one or both parents after the divorce. The parents played on their children's sympathy, tried to get information about the other parent, told untrue things about the other parent, and sought to involve the children in continuing quarrels."[6] Trauma after divorce may be less in children coming from unhappy homes than in those from homes that seemed to be happy. Studies of delinquency indicate that more children who get into trouble come from divorced homes

---

[5] Gerald Leslie, *The Family in Social Context.* New York: Oxford University Press, 1976.
[6] Ibid.

than from intact families; however, the percentage spread is not great.

Region and Other Factors

Urban areas tend to have higher divorce rates than rural areas. Urban living conditions tend to stimulate divorce, and there is also a tendency for divorced persons to move to cities. City life offers more opportunities for singles to develop a social life. The style of rural and suburban areas tends to be geared to the needs of the married.

"Divorce rates increase from east to west across the country, reflecting differences in attitudes and values, and in the age, ethnic, and religious composition of the population. The relative divorce rates among whites and blacks have been changing. As blacks have come to rely less on separation, their divorce rates have been rising rapidly and now exceed those of whites. A greater proportion of blacks are found in the lower socioeconomic strata, and there is an inverse correlation between socioeconomic status and divorce rates. Whether occupation, education, or income is used as the criterion of economic status, the relationships hold." [7]

A number of studies show that more separations occur during the first year of marriage than in any other year. The next peak figure occurs from the second to the fourth year. Then divorces decline until the seventh or eighth year of the marriage. Some researchers assert that first marriages last longer than remarriages. Some divorce lawyers feel that as many second as first marriages end in divorce.

Desertion often precedes divorce. Catholic desertion rates are higher than those of other groups, because the Catholic Church makes divorce very difficult to obtain. In the past, men tended to be the ones to desert their families. Recent studies, however, show that more and more women are deserting their husbands, which means that a new social problem—especially as it affects children—may be emerging. As more and more women go to work and gain equal rights, it is not surprising that the differences in conduct between men and women diminish.

Another striking finding of researchers is that husbands usually are the first to want a divorce, but they maneuver their wives into asking for it. Some recent studies (not accepted by all researchers) indicate that most divorced women do not feel discriminated against

---

[7] Ibid.

as divorcees, that in the long run most keep former friends and are able to cope financially, and, most important, the majority remarry. Such studies must be approached with a degree of caution. Other studies have shown a severe trauma, loss of friends, and nagging financial problems when divorce occurs. It may be that in the long run most divorced wives are able to readjust and reestablish their lives, but this may take time and the emotional scars often remain for years and—in many cases—forever.

Statistics and You

As a person, you are much more than a statistic. If we were to live by what statistics project, no one would marry, since the odds on success seem to be getting worse and worse. Yet people do fall in love and marry. They bring children into the world, and they do find a measure of happiness. All that statistics can do is to present a history of what has happened up to the present. They can give us some idea of what is ahead, but they are not infallible. For example, all present research would say that the baby boom of the 1950's cannot occur again. People are not statistics, however, and they do not jump through a hoop held by a computer. Any projections for the future can only be based on probability. Variables enter the picture, together with the whims of human emotion. Suppose young couples suddenly get turned on to large families? At the moment a new baby "boomlette" has emerged.

In the 1960's and early 1970's the young people of America were radicalized, and the generation gap grew very wide. Youth today tend to be less rebellious and much more conservative in their thinking. Change is the one constant in human life. Attitudes toward marriage and divorce are not fixed in one orbit of thought. Youth are more serious about marriage. They live together because they want to be certain that, if they do wed, the marriage will be viable. Having seen many failures in their parents' generation, as well as the high incidence of breakup among their contemporaries, they may well be ushering in a new era in which greater care in mate selection takes place. Statistics indicate that usually the better educated are less likely to divorce. As more and more of the population—men and women—obtain advanced educational degrees, the trend toward divorce may be slowed. Social scientists are perplexed by the results they are finding. On the one hand, they find a segment of society that takes marriage somewhat lightly. On the other hand, they find many young couples determined to make their marriages work and prosper. Delayed parenthood may be evidence of a strong inclination to make certain that they can get along well with their mates. The question of bringing children into the world is approached with the greatest seriousness.

Statistics show that there is a variety of reasons—open and hidden—why marriages fail. Fewer studies are made of the happy marriages that succeed. Divorce is very "in" today, and statistics show that the sociology of divorce makes it another acceptable life-style in our mobile and ever-changing American culture. In my own work I detect a somewhat different emerging pattern. People seem to be less flippant about marriage. If I ask a couple, "Is this your first marriage?" they often answer—with some indignation—"Yes, this is our first and last marriage. We intend to have a successful marriage. Nothing will stop us from succeeding." I have also found that more and more young persons are adding original vows to the marriage ceremony, and they recite these vows to each other. One bride spoke these words to her beloved:

> Your mildness
>   leaves me in awe
> just as your strength
>   makes me wonder
>   with open eye
>   and open heart
> what gift could I give you?
> what treasure would be worthy?
> what madness is within me
>   that would make me suffer
> a child's first pain
>   one-thousand fold
> if you should ever leave me
> that I would die in your arms
>   before I love in another's

The bride who spoke those words was young in years. The depth of her feelings was crystal clear. She is not likely to be divorced a few years from today.

Thought Questions

1. Do you think statistics are helpful in understanding divorce?
2. Can statistics be helpful to a person confronting divorce? Can they be detrimental?

3. Do you think that the divorce laws in America are fair? Why or why not?
4. How would you change the divorce laws, if you had the power to do so?
5. Should statistics on the rising rate of divorce make couples think seriously before getting married?
6. Do you think that divorce statistics will slow the marriage rate? Why or why not?

CHAPTER II

Attitudes

We are socialized to one day stand at the altar or before a justice of the peace. Marriage is as American as motherhood and apple pie. Despite the inroads of the women's rights movement, marriage is here to stay, and the feminists themselves do not discount its value. They speak constantly of the need for open marriage, where each partner has a wide measure of freedom and self-expression. The antimarriage forces say that marriage is only one possibility amid a wide variety of choices. In an earlier age, if you did not wed, you were either a confirmed bachelor or an old maid. Today, you can go through life as a single and be considered a career person. The unwed are no longer considered peculiar. Many would say that they have merely elected a particular life-style.

Challenges to Contemporary Values

At one time you not only were expected to marry, but it was also assumed that you would have children. The childless marriage was anathema to society. Eager in-laws would pressure the couple until the first child was born. Today, there are organizations of childless couples who rejoice in this status. When pressed, they declare that children ruin a marriage, since the love of parents must now be shared with children, who are an intrusion into a formerly happy home. Some proclaim that not all are fit to be parents. Far too many children are not wanted after they are born. Parents are "stuck" with them, because society demands that families have children. Some who live together decide to wed so that maternity insurance benefits can be utilized. Much of society does not countenance "living together" and looks with little favor upon the childless family.

Attitudes Toward Marriage

I frequently begin my college course on The Family by asking the students how many of them plan to make a 50-year commitment on their wedding day. Usually I am greeted with a stunned silence. Then hands go up. "Dr. Raab, you must be kidding." "How can anyone be sure how she will feel 50 years from now?" "I could never think of being in love with the same person for 50 years." "With today's divorce rate, I cannot be that certain about anything. How do I know I will be alive tomorrow?" The almost unanimous verdict of my students is that no one can be really that sure about marriage. A few in the class do say that they are making a 50-year pledge, but they are usually the older students or some of the youngest ones who admit still being idealistic and romantic. "Dr. Raab, I am of the old school. I know I will make my marriage work. If it fails, then it is my fault." One mature student said, "On my wedding day I knew it would last, and it has. We have both changed, but we are still together."

Invariably the question of commitment leads to comments about the prevalence of divorce. "My parents are divorced. I would be a fool to expect my own marriage to survive for 50 years." Having seen failure at home, many young people enter marriage with decidedly lower expectations.

"Even if we both work at it, who is to say that our marriage will make it?"

It is somewhat disconcerting to teach young people who lack faith in themselves as well as in the institution of marriage. If nothing else, they are certainly realists. Since we are told that the divorce rate may be approaching one in every two marriages, a survival rate of 50 percent is not very encouraging. Also, some young people are the products of "blended" families, meaning that they are being raised by stepparents. Such a "reconstituted" family faces additional pressures. The cry of a ten-year-old girl: "You are not my real mother, so you cannot tell me to clean up my room" does not make for stability in a second marriage. Frequently one hears such statements as, "It is not easy trying to get her kids and my kids to live together peacefully under one roof, especially when her former husband spoils her children so much."

The Traditional Marriage

There was a time when couples promised to love, honor, and obey forever. In some marriage vows were the words, "until death do us part." Today, it seems that togetherness exists only so long as the needs of each partner are fulfilled. The use of the word partner, in current parlance, is a further indication of new directions. No one is a boss in the modern home. We have partners. And when partners quarrel, they may split up. A generation ago, people entered into marriage with the belief that the marriage must succeed. Expectations were not so high. There was less emphasis on physical love. Marriage had, as a major function, the preservation of society. You married so as to bring children into the world and take care of them. If you and your mate were truly compatible, that was an extra bonus. The accent was less on happiness than on duty. It was a duty to wed, form a home, have children, educate them, and then in old age enjoy the grandchildren. On your wedding day, you could see your whole life stretch before you. Chances were that you expected to live in the same town for the rest of your life, to keep many of the same friends. You expected to share responsibilities, but they were carefully delineated. The male was the breadwinner; the female was the wife, mother, and housekeeper. The male was the head of the household. Whatever he earned was to be sufficient. He would have the largest say in how money was to be spent. A wife could look at her own mother and see what she would be doing some thirty years hence. There was not much mystery about life. We fell naturally into place in the cycle of what was normal and expected.

In some countries this pattern persists. Although there are some signs of emancipation in Japan, girls there are expected to marry young and have children. It is an unwritten rule that no woman over age 35 works; clerks in the stores are invariably young women in their late teens or twenties. Traditional marriage forms still persist in much of the world. It is primarily in the Western nations that women play a more equal role in the home and in the work force. Consciousness-raising for women is largely an American phenomenon. I recall attending a conference in Israel a number of years ago. We were addressed by an old-line Zionist leader, who made the mistake of asserting that woman's place was in the home. He was roundly booed by his American listeners, who did not take kindly to this expression of male chauvinism. It should be noted that even in a youth-oriented society like the state of Israel women are still expected to marry young and become mothers and housekeepers. The working career wife who carries an equal share of the financial burden remains basically a Western phenomenon.

Devitalized Relationships

Americans pride themselves on vitality. Young couples are frequently athletically inclined. The young will bowl, play golf, enjoy tennis, and in general share in athletic skills and pursuits. Ours is a culture that glorifies the body and the skills in sports. We want to have fun with our friends and lovers. Enthusiasm and dynamism are the measure of individual strength and growth. As in the past, young couples tend to be very much in love as they stand before their clergyperson. The wedding party often exhibits a tremendous outpouring of good spirits. The bride, groom, and wedding guests often "dance up a storm." As one watches them whirling on the dance floor, one wonders how they will act five months from today. Will they still hold hands and look into each other's eyes with ardor and affection? Will they truly care about each other and be concerned, helpful, and attentive? Or will they slip into a pattern of dull sameness, broken only by quarrels or long silences that bode only trouble? The "I'm accustomed to my fate" marriage is found in many homes. Neither partner has the energy to seek divorce. Besides, divorce costs money, and they sort of like being together.

"Now that Joe is gone, I find I miss him. I just cannot stand being alone. It is true that he seldom spoke when he was home. I know that he was unfaithful. Of course, I was not the best wife either. I never really enjoyed sex with him. But it sure is lonely. I work during the day, but I dread coming home to an empty house. You have no idea how awful it is. When the children were young, even if our relationship was not great, we still had the kids. Raising them took up most of my time and energy. Joe was around, and he was a good father. Now that the nest is empty and we really have to look at each other, we find we are worlds apart. Joe has moved out. In a way I cannot blame him. Our marriage got to be very 'blah.' We scarcely spoke to each other. Maybe it would have been better if we had shown anger. Our marriage lost its vitality. There must have been something—way back—in the beginning. Whatever it was, it sure got lost along the way." The woman begins to weep. The vital juices have been drained from her relationship with her husband. He is off with a new companion. She says, "How can I, at my age, start hanging around bars? Men can always get a young chick. Who will show any interest in me?"

The devitalized marriage has a quality of desperation about it. The marriage does not dissolve all at once; it happens over a period of time. The couple begin to drift apart. The devitalized marriage may be a marriage of convenience. "I tolerate my husband's infidelity. Does that surprise you? It should not. I still maintain his name. I live in the home with the children. In time, I feel he will come back to me. He has been chasing women for years. It is not a pleasant situation, and I know that my friends are gossiping behind my back. Many of them have urged me to make a break. He is a wealthy man, and I am sure I would not have any money problems if we were to divorce. But what would I be? At my age can I start dating? Do I want to play the role of the gay divorcée? That would be ridiculous. Besides, in time he will come back to me. He has come back to me in the past. I will not sue for divorce, even though that is obviously what he wants. So we will continue to play our little game of husband-and-wife. I really do not have any good alternative. Sure, we have a marriage that is not much of a marriage. I was raised to hold on. To my generation, divorce is a sign of failure. Besides, what would my children think? Even though they are fully grown, it would devastate them. They idolize their father. Can I bring them such heartbreak? Besides, who in this world is really happy. Why do we place such stress on happiness?" The woman has a point. Our culture is very much based on the concept of happiness.

Make Me Happy

If there is one word we hear at weddings, it is happiness. "All I want is for the kids to be happy." This sentiment is heard over and over again on the wedding day—if only they will be happy. But if they are not happy, who is to blame? At one time, the failure of a marriage was a reflection on the parents. "How can I face my friends when they hear that my son is getting divorced? The wedding was only five months ago, and it cost a small fortune. Now the kids are separated. It is so hard to confide to friends that the divorce is imminent. When I am asked about the kids, I just smile and say they're fine. What else am I going to say? It is no one's business. They seemed so happy at the wedding. I wonder what went wrong. Maybe we raised our son with the wrong ideas. Could we be at fault?"

Some schools of psychology blame the parents for the sins of the children. So, by extension, if the marriage fails, it is because the child did not receive the proper kind of loving while growing up, thus making the child unfit to wed. He was not capable of showing and receiving affection. He was flawed—and it was our fault as parents.

The happiness syndrome is very much with us. I want to be happy. Today you make me happy because you are my wife and you care about me. Tomorrow I do not love you because you just do not turn me on. So I will look for someone who can make me feel good. The accent is on "me." A certain narcissistic tone is heard. My needs come first. One wonders why we stress happiness so much? Previous generations were glad just to survive. The raising and educating of children was sufficient. Individual fulfillment was fine if it happened to exist. If you were not that happy, then—so what? Most of your friends were not ecstatic either. Most marriages were day-to-day accustomed-to-my-fate relationships. Whoever said that you have to be filled with joy?

Young people certainly want to be satisfied and feel that things are going well. Their parents seem dedicated to making them happy. Their wishes and needs are gratified—often before they are uttered. The commercials on television point to instant gratification. Children are not taught to be obedient; an obedient American child is an oddity. Foreign children who are adopted often undergo culture shock. They are not used to the permissiveness of the typical American home. There is precious little discipline. Parents are pals. Kids are taught to express themselves.

It is not the same everywhere. In Scandinavia one sees respect shown for people and for property. In some foreign lands, you can rent land, grow vegetables, and know that no one will steal them when your back is turned. On a two-week trip through Norway, Sweden, and Denmark, we did not see one policeman in uniform on the streets. Yet we walked freely at night, without fear. The local folk said there was very little crime. The children seemed well adjusted, laughing, and happy, yet they did not run wild. Scandinavians do a lot for the children. Cities are filled with parks where children play freely. At concerts in the parks, the children are often moved forward to sit in front of the adults. Children are catered to, but it does not make them wild or disrespectful.

Our society certainly needs some self-inspection. The individuality we prize in the "frontier" spirit of America may have led to a type of narcissistic behavior—what I want and what makes me happy is the be-all and end-all of life. Perhaps in just the casual act of dropping a gum wrapper on the street we are saying, "Let someone else pick it up. That is what we pay street cleaners for." It may involve a lack of pride and an attitude that shouts to the world, "I will do what I wish to do."

Person-ness is important. Not to respect yourself can be damaging. But a person who comes to believe that the whole world must cater to him or her is not a good candidate for any lasting relationship. For a relationship to be viable, each must be willing to give. Marriages cannot survive if we expect total happiness. And if we expect our mates always to give while we receive, danger signs are on the horizon.

In a good marriage there are shared goals, dreams, and desires. There is also a sense of respect for the other person and his or her wishes. We must allow our mates room to grow and give them "living space."

Realistic expectations should be found in relationships. Both partners to a marriage should find a degree of fulfillment. Life can be challenging and stimulating. Good interaction and communication can make for excitement and enrichment. A sharing of goals can be

satisfying to both husband and wife. In a good marriage, the sense
of excitement is never dissipated. In times of stress, the family pulls
together, rather than apart.

I spoke to a family that was going through a terrible financial
crisis. Business reverses were so bad that they felt they might lose
their home. Twenty years of striving seemed about to go down the
drain. The parents were in good health, and their children were a
source of great happiness. In this awful crisis, it was beautiful to see
how supportive they were of each other. The wife continued to be
loving. She reassured her husband that he had really done the best
he could. She exuded confidence that everything would turn out just
fine. She gave her husband the will to do his best, and, even more
vital, she gave him the room to fail. He knew that he would not be
condemned for failure. She made it clear she had confidence in him
and that eventually they would work things out. She never lost a
sense of vitality. Her eyes sparkled with love. If she had condemned
him and called him stupid for his failed business, the man would
have been crushed. As it was, this family was able to weather the
storm and even find a degree of happiness, despite the awful economic pressures that might have destroyed their marriage.

So we see that good marriages can exist in situations where there
is genuine economic distress, and bad marriages fall apart even
though money is not the problem.

Happiness requires many things. Money certainly helps, but fi-
nances are not the only cause of a breakdown. Emotional factors
are vital. Selfishness can wreck more marriages than financial reverses. Happiness does not exist in a vacuum. The person who is a
taker and expects everyone to slave to make him happy is not likely
to find much fulfillment.

Thought Questions

1. Has your attitude toward marriage been changed by reading this
   chapter?
2. How do you react to a devitalized marriage? Do you think such
   marriages are in the majority?
3. How important is it for your mate to make you happy, once you
   are married?
4. Is happiness something that comes automatically in marriage?
   How hard must people work to make their marriage a success?
5. Who do you think is usually to blame when a divorce occurs?

CHAPTER III

Marriage

People often speak of the ideal marriage. One wonders if it really exists. What is ideal for one couple might not be so for another. Some enter into marriage with the greatest expectations, looking forward to a life shared with a loving, caring, sympathetic partner who will always be responsive to their needs and expectations. The idealized approach to marriage finds its way into novels, plays, and books. Yet society's fascination with the "problem" marriage may give a clue to the inner notion that we do not believe there really is an ideal marriage. If this were true, there would be only one person in the whole wide world for you. In actual fact, you could be happy with a great variety of persons. In order to wed, you are geographically limited. Some sociologists hold that you will marry a person who lives within a 20-block radius of your address when you are at the most marriageable age, say between age 18 and 28.

To speak of the ideal means we expect perfection. But marriages are formed by people, and all of us are flawed. We have our individual likes, dislikes, opinions, needs, and desires. If there is a mutuality of expectations, the marriage does have a good chance of success.

As a young person, you may be dating a variety of partners, each with some strengths and some weaknesses. A girl may be a great dancer but a poor conversationalist. A boy may be awkward and clumsy, yet his intelligence attracts you. Seldom are all the virtues found in the same person. There is a reality factor to be considered. The tragedy is that what may attract us at age 25 becomes unbearable at age 45. The qualities we seek in a mate in our 20's may not stand the test of time—which is, after all, the ultimate measure of the viability of the relationship. A girl may marry the quarterback of the college football team and then discover in time that they have little in common outside of physical attraction to each other.

It might be better to consider the ingredients that go into a good marriage. We may strive for the ideal, but always we should be aware that the ideal is beyond achievement.

The good marriage is based upon mutual faith and trust. Some of the ingredients can now be considered.

Love

It is written in the Bible (Ecclesiastes 9:9), "Thou shalt enjoy life with the woman thou lovest." Joy is not extraneous to life. A couple should give each other pleasure. When pleasing your mate, you will also please yourself. A major purpose of life is to enrich our lives. A couple who are in love can inspire each other. Love does make the world go round, and we can often achieve the impossible if our mate has confidence in us. Love is more than sexual attraction, although a vital ingredient of marriage is sexual compatibility. Love includes sex and so much more. There is the sharing of special moments and the nearness of someone who really cares. Love can involve sacrifice. We may give up some temporary pleasure so that we can please our mate. This need not demean or diminish us. Much of love involves the willingness to give as well as to receive. Selfish love is demanding.

We are long past the stage where the woman is the obedient mistress, hanging on every word of her lord and master. The male does not have absolute power. Love cannot be used as a weapon to demand obedience. It is also to be noted, however, that some wives use love as a means of reward or punishment. If the husband is nice, they will tolerate love-making. If not, they withdraw into a shell. One young divorcée told me, "I forced Arthur to seek a divorce. I refused to have sex with him for a full year. He finally got the message that our marriage was over." Love should not be utilized for either reward or punishment. It should flow gently and naturally, as part of the harmony of a good relationship.

Love and sex are not always the same. The physical act of coitus is usually most satisfactory within the marriage bed. Today, young people do have premarital sex, and some couples live together before taking their marriage vows. Such nontraditional arrangements are increasing, especially among the young. Having seen so much divorce among family and friends, they have decided to try it first. This trial period of living together does not always indicate what the future will bring. Unfortunately, many of those who live together have seen the relationship dissolve after the wedding vows are spoken: "When we were living together, it was him and me against them. It was great. We avoided our parents. We had each other and worked hard to make the relationship a success. We really were out to prove that we could live together. Then we got married. Soon we had in-law problems. Money difficulties also cropped up. It is amazing that just by signing a little slip of paper we put the stamp of doom on our feelings. I wonder why?"

The preceding lament or variations of it are heard often. It is not enough to say "I love you." It is not even enough to have "good sex" with another person. Love involves more than that. There has to be a sharing of feelings and a response to the needs of one's partner. Love is not total giving or total receiving. In its finest sense, it fosters respect, admiration, and a desire to be with another person.

Love begins with strong physical attraction. It will persist if it matures into a good relationship where two people care deeply and are willing to work at sustaining it. Love is not a gift; rather it is an achievement. It can slip away because of neglect, harsh words, selfishness, and abuse. The unfaithful mate is making a statement; he or she is saying, "I can be totally free in every way." Few marriages can withstand sexual infidelity. Human jealousy being what it is, how can a marriage be solid and secure if one partner strays continually? We can share many experiences with our mates. Our interests may diverge where sports, theatre, music, and the arts are concerned. But when a married man or woman has coitus outside marriage, a statement is being made. That person is saying, "You do not satisfy me, so I must go elsewhere. Or, "I am bored. You are not a good lover." Or, "This is my way of saying that you ignore me. If you will not make me an important part of your life, then I will find someone else who will." The neglected spouse may turn to others for sexual excitement. When this happens, the marriage is in deep trouble.

Poets have spoken of love as a seal upon the arm and heart. The arm is a symbol of action. Love must be executed; it cannot be passive. Marriages die when the partners look upon sex as a duty rather than a pleasure. If love is truly a seal upon the heart, then it deals with our gut feelings—with our deepest emotions. A good marriage requires action (the seal upon the arm) and feeling (the seal upon the heart). From the feelings deep within us will arise the actions leading to love.

We can show love in many ways other than sex. By a loving act we can give support to someone who feels discouraged or downhearted. The sensitive mate is attuned to his partner's feelings and needs. Just being there and helping can also express love. Our love is not a constant litany of saying, "I love you." True, the words are important, and they should be said frequently; but we demonstrate by our manner, our helpfulness, our sympathy and support that we truly love another person. Our lover should also be our friend. In the best of marriages, the partners not only love one another, they like each other, too. They are able to be friends. Some relationships begin with friendship and develop into love: "Mary and I were good friends. We used to discuss our problems together. We would even talk about our girlfriends and boyfriends. Then, one day, we suddenly began to see that we did not just like each other as friends. Something deeper and more meaningful was emerging. Our relationship ripened into love. I cannot tell you exactly when this happened. It just did. And we are very excited about it. We like each other—and we are also beginning to love each other. That is a combination that cannot be beat." These words were spoken in a rush of enthusiasm by a young man who brought his fiancée to me to talk about marriage. As I looked at them I had the feeling that theirs would be a vital and lasting marriage. After the young man spoke, his fiancée said, "Harold and I really like each other. We respect each other. We have both known what it is to struggle to get where we are. Harold did not have an easy time of it, getting accepted to dental school; he had to get his M.S. first. He is older than many of the students in his class. My parents could not afford to pay for my education. To get a B.A., I had to work and take out college loans. It will be years before those loans are paid back. We know the value of a dollar and how hard it is to make it financially. We have had many shared experiences. We find we are thinking on the same wavelength. Though we occasionally quarrel, we kiss and make up because we respect each other. We are in love—and we are friends, too." When couples speak this way, you have the intuitive feeling that their marriage will endure.

The Front

Some couples are excellent actors and actresses. When they are out in society, with friends, they put on a good act. They pretend that all is well. When their marriage crumbles, people say, "I never would have thought it could happen. They were the most together couple in our crowd." In actual fact, the only time their marriage was bearable was when they were out with their friends. You do not bicker in front of friends. They were not compatible at all, but they could play-act in the marriage game.

No one knows what goes on behind closed doors, but that is the true test of whether a relationship is viable. Public displays, even of affection, count for very little. It is not enough to make a game of love. To smile and hug in public is fine if it is sincere, but too often such conduct is a cover-up for problems that are being faced privately and often not successfully.

A very wise rabbi in the Talmud (Avoth 2.11) is credited with saying that the good wife is a good friend. We might add that the good husband must also be a good friend. Marriage does not exist in the world of "let's pretend." Marriage cannot endure if one face is shown to the public while at home there is continuous dissent.

Another religious teacher said, "Who are real lovers? They who have one heart in two bodies" (Zabara: Sefer Shaashuim 307). The teacher is telling us that two who are very much in love find that their hearts are attuned to each other so that it is almost as if they shared the same heart. Such a notion may seem overly romantic in a time when we stress individuality and respect for the other person. Marriage is often looked upon as a place where there is freedom to grow. This can be fine if that freedom allows the partner also to be free and to develop. When we constrict our mates and hem them in, then love fades—only to flicker fitfully at public gatherings where it is necessary to put on an act before our friends.

Love Is Shared

When a couple stand at the marriage altar, there is an awareness that it is not just their own love that they bring to the occasion. The love of families and friends mingles with theirs and thus adds a special dimension to the moment. Love does not exist by itself. It must want others to participate in it. The joyous sounds of the wedding celebration show that shared experiences can be very fulfilling to the participants, and this shared moment is not private. The community of family, friends, and well-wishers are present. Love needs to be proclaimed, not hidden, and in the declaration comes the sense of obligation. What we declare publicly, we will tend to observe privately. At the wedding, the guests are there to see the public recitation of the couple's marriage vows. At that point, family and friends become important. The marriage ceremony demands a certain ritual and pageantry. Few are satisfied with a perfunctory recital of vows. The reason families go into debt to provide their children with big expensive weddings is not easy to explain. It may be because of social custom, or the family may feel that they will look cheap if they do not have a lavish affair. Yet it may simply be a desire to invite all of one's friends and relatives to a celebration. It may also be that the parents secretly hope that through such a public display the children will feel more of an obligation to make the marriage work. No parents should contract for a lavish wedding on the premise that such a display will give the couple pause if trouble develops later. Far too many parents have learned to their grief that they are paying the wedding costs months after the marriage has dissolved. A big wedding is no guarantee that the couple will live happily ever after. The size of the wedding has little relationship to the success of the couple in making their marriage a lasting and loving experience.

Love as Magic

Only the foolish would expect love to solve all of one's problems. If you enter into marriage in the belief that love will totally transform you and your partner, be aware that dangers are ahead. Love can intensify positive attributes; it may even hide or disguise faults for a time. But the true personality of the person remains. No amount of love can alter our basic natures. Love can bring to the fore our best qualities, provided that they exist. The words "I love you" imply commitment. That is why your partner is so eager to hear them. It is one thing to say that you are fond of a person or that you like him or her. A declaration of love is taken with seriousness. In a religious ceremony you may be asked if you agree to love, honor, and cherish your partner. This public declaration shows a strong desire to do so. Still, one cannot spell out what love is. Individuals may define it in different ways. Ultimately, we are saying that we care very deeply for another human being. In marriage, we agree to share our entire life with that person. It is implied that we will show fidelity to our mate. We will be together in both good and difficult times. The strength of our feelings for our mate will go a long way toward helping us weather whatever storms may arise in life.

Love is the special ingredient that makes everything else happen. Where love is gone, the marriage either dissolves or degenerates into a mundane relationship of convenience. When we are first in love, we may act in a rather dazed manner, but in time life has to come into focus. Love has to mature and grow as the years come and go. Love will be subjected to many strains and stresses. Some of the magic may wear thin when the baby is born and the mother cannot devote full attention to her mate. Financial reverses can bring a strain to the relationship. In-law problems are common. A host of situations can put pressure on initial feelings of affection. Love is magic to the extent that we strive diligently to make a success of our marriage. Fits of rage, sulking, terrible silences—all of these are ominous portents. Love is destroyed when we are quick to criticize and find fault. Few torrid romances can stand the strain of infidelity and neglect. Love is effective if we use it as a tool to make our marriage grow and blossom. It is part of the process of living together. Like a plant that needs water to survive, a marriage must be fed with the flowing stream of love if it is to blossom into what the partners are seeking. The magic is in us, and not in the word love.

No Guarantees

If you sign a written document agreeing to love a person, that paper may be legally binding, but it can never be emotionally binding. The climbing divorce statistics give us pause for concern. Public vows of affection are soon forgotten in the welter of recriminations and heartache that flows from an unstable marriage. Poets speak of love, but they are expressing hope—they cannot guarantee realization. Dreams can be fulfilled if there is tenderness and caring. If there is jealousy and possessiveness and unreasonableness, then marriages dissolve. Love can help us grow emotionally. It is there to evoke the desire to "kiss and make up." Continual quarrels will lead to a break-up. There are no performance guarantees in marriage. Every relationship involves a certain amount of risk. Marriage is a high-risk arrangement, since it places two different persons in a situation where they are to share their lives. Some have said it is amazing that two out of four marriages actually survive. Do not be discouraged because one of two marriages fail; rather be grateful that half have a measure of success. Love does not guarantee that your marriage will work, but if you begin without a true sense of affection, trouble will follow. Love is the strong foundation upon which you can build for the future. If love is absent, the marriage has only a slim chance. I am not impressed by those who say, "Well, you can grow to love him in time." This is not likely. Begin with love. From it, all else can develop.

Understanding

Another basic ingredient in a good marriage is understanding. It implies that we have an open, accepting attitude toward our mate. The gift of understanding is precious. It can make the difference between success and failure. It is recorded in the Bible that Solomon was offered anything he wished. He told God, "Give me an understanding heart." Develop the willingness to say, "Yes, I understand how you feel and how you think. Let us talk things over. If I do not fully understand, then please explain your ideas to me again, and I will try to do better." This is what understanding is all about. "I can see that you are tired tonight, so we do not have to go to visit our friends." Such a statement can put our partner at ease. Understanding gives our partners room to maneuver. We do not box them in with demands and restrictions. Understanding shows that we care enough to consider someone else's feelings and desires.

In a good marriage, this wise approach can help us over many bumps. If we can truly listen and discuss, our understanding heart shines through.

Understanding is more than an intellectual exercise. It is in the realm of emotion. Some people are brilliant at understanding the most complicated mathematical formulas, yet they can be totally deficient in their approach to the simplest human problem. A woman once complained, "My husband is a brilliant scientist. He is well respected by his colleagues. They flock to his lectures. His mind is in the genius category. Yet in the simple problems of everyday life we have little or no communication. He refuses to assume any responsibility around the house. I am constantly exasperated by his attitude. He just does not understand that I, too, can become tired and restless. I am his wife, but I often have the feeling that I am more like a maid than a wife. What can I do to get him to be more understanding of my needs?" This can be a serious defect in a relationship. A refusal to understand, even when your partner cries out to you to listen, can destroy the marriage. Communication is vital to sustain the relationship.

As a young person you may have wished that your parents were more understanding. You hoped that they would see your point of view. If they would not agree, you at least hoped that they would listen to you. It is an insult to a child not to listen. It is destructive of a marriage to yawn and be inattentive to the cry for help from your mate: "I never thought she would ask for a divorce. Everyone said we had the best marriage in our crowd. Suddenly she said she could not take it any longer. I make a good living. I have provided for her needs. I know she gets restless and bored. I have to be away frequently on trips, but unless I travel we cannot maintain our present standard of living. I always thought she understood my problems. Now she wants a separation. She says she needs time to think. She says that I do not understand her. What is there to understand? I know that I have to work hard. Often at night I am just too tired to talk to her or to play with the children. I would do more, but I am just not physically able. She should try to understand me and my situation."

Statements such as this show that a family is rapidly growing apart, rather than together. The husband sees himself as the provider and he expects his wife to be wife and mother. His view follows the traditionalist pattern of husband as breadwinner, with a minimum of other responsibilities. Today we live in a world of shared concerns. That is why marriage is called a partnership. In such a marriage, the husband has to find the time to be with his wife and children. Money, vital as it is, is not the end-all of a relationship. What good is money if you are too tired to enjoy it? What is the value of becoming head of the company if it destroys your marriage? Priorities are changing. The new psychology is saying that if we are truly understanding perhaps we have to settle for less in the way of worldly possessions while seeking greater opportunities for contact with our families. Increasingly it becomes apparent that we cannot have it both ways. Since our society glorifies competition and being a winner, the male or female who rises to the top of the corporate heap may leave a trail of broken marriages in his or her wake.

Today young people may say, "We do not intend to have children. It is just too expensive." When we realize that it may cost as much as $80,000 to raise and educate one child, there is reason to pause and think. An earlier generation did not count the cost. If you wanted children, you brought them into the world. The child was not an economic statistic; it would be loved and cared for as best you could. Conventional wisdom says that the size of families must be limited, and the earth's ecology may demand this. But the childless couple who refrain from bringing kids into the world because of economics may be far off base. Who is truly wise? My answer would be that person who has a compassionate heart. Wisdom is not measured in how much money you earn.

What is important is to try to understand your mate. The effort is important. You can say, "I do not fully see why you want to do this, but I am willing to listen to you. Would you explain it to me again? I may be a little thick, but your ideas just do not ring a bell." It is not always what you say that counts. Your tone of voice and your desire to understand can be critical.

The trouble comes when couples do not say what is on their minds. Understanding demands a degree of openness. Where there is fear, understanding goes out the window. The desire not to disturb your mate is seldom the best course of action. It has been said that the best time to discuss problems is after having a satisfying meal. At that point, people are more relaxed, and intelligent discussion of a problem can take place.

Faith

A good marriage demands a degree of faith. You have to believe in yourself, as well as in your partner. You have to respect your partner as a person in his or her own right. Respect and faith go hand in hand. You have to realize that both of you will make mistakes. You may even fail, on many occasions, to fully resolve difficulties. But if you have faith that things will work out when there is team effort, your chances of succeeding are enhanced. Your partner will quickly sense whether or not you have faith. "Bill never believed I could do anything. When I wanted to continue going to college after we were married, he said, 'Why bother? I am making enough to take care of both of us. Enjoy yourself. Don't burden yourself with college. Isn't it enough that you take care of the house and of me? When will you find time to study? You know I am not handy in the kitchen. What will we do about meals if you are rushing off to evening classes? Besides, when will we get to see each other? Sure, Kathy, I have faith in you. I know you are capable. But we haven't been married that long. I really need to have you around at night when I get home from work. Let's talk about this another time'." In such a situation, the husband shows his own lack of faith in himself. He does not wish to have his routine interrupted. Bill has a fixed image of what a wife should be. He wants a happy little homemaker, bustling around the kitchen. He did not marry such a person. Perhaps his wife started out to be the homebody but soon grew bored and restless. Now she wants to go to college. Bill lacks faith in her sense of proportion, and he is unsure of himself. He fears that if they do not have dinner together a vital ingredient of the marriage will be lost. His wife has confidence that she can go to school and also attend to the household chores. Bill is a young husband, and he feels that in the first years of marriage they should be together a maximum amount of time. As the couple establish strong bonds of communication, they demonstrate their faith in each other. If you believe in someone, you come to respect that person's wisdom and judgment. In a good marriage the partners have faith in each other. They really believe that the relationship will remain exciting and vital. The wife traditionally was expected to have faith that the husband would succeed in his job; the husband was to have confidence that the wife would be a good mother and housekeeper. These traditional goals are being modified as women demand their rights and the economic squeeze intensifies. Women work not only out of desire, but often out of necessity. The high cost of living has resulted in over one-third of the labor force being female. In such a world women will be spending less and less time in the home. Can problems of the use of time be worked out? With a degree of optimism the matters can be resolved, but it takes faith and confidence in your partner.

A good marriage is one in which the couple has faith in the future. They believe that all problems can be confronted and either resolved or lived with. Maturity teaches us that not every problem has an answer. Some difficulties are built into certain situations and simply have to be endured. In life, we learn to live with partial success and less than satisfactory answers. With faith, we are confident that some sort of solution will result, and we can evolve a degree of happiness and fulfillment. Deep faith in the integrity of the other members of the family can be a lifesaver. If you have faith in your partner, he will sense it. Faith is difficult to define. It means that we really believe in someone else. That faith tends to persevere under the most trying situations. One of the beautiful things in a good marriage is the ability to be supportive of your mate in times of trouble. Faith cannot cure sickness, but the doctors tell us that a patient who knows that others believe he will get well may have a better chance to recover.

Faith allows a couple to share their concern when their child is ill. It is hard to go it alone when a family crisis arises. When there is trust, no matter what occurs we know that others stand by us. Even if the situation turns out badly, we have someone to talk to in the aftermath. There is great comfort in knowing that someone else has respect for our judgment. Faith means to believe in something or someone. For the religious, it may mean that faith in God will help a person to overcome his fears. Faith alone cannot do everything. With human effort, faith can almost "move the mountains" of doubt and despair. Faith may involve such a mundane matter as giving us the confidence to try, knowing that if we fail we will not be condemned. The courage to try with the knowledge that win or lose we will not be rejected—this is vital to most people.

Truly Good?

If a marriage is to be classified as "good," it should be good for both partners. At times one partner may be quite comfortable in the marriage. A husband may be well satisfied with the way things are going. His wife is at home and takes care of the children. She entertains beautifully when he brings clients home for dinner. The house is neat and clean. When he comes home a hot meal is ready to be put on the table. After dinner he relaxes in front of the television set while his wife does the dishes. Later his dutiful mate trundles the children up to their bedrooms. His wife is attentive to his needs and interested in what concerns him the most. Why should such a man be unhappy? He may not realize that what is very comfortable for him is hell for his wife. She may long to get a part-time job. She is secretly angry that he never lifts a finger to help around the house. She may be exhausted from a grueling routine taking care of the young children. Such a husband may be in for a rude awakening when his wife finally tells him what is wrong. Such a confrontation can either be a cleansing for both parties, or it can lead to marital disaster.

A good marriage is good for both spouses. This is not to say that we do not find marriages in which the wife really enjoys her role as a homemaker. Not every woman wishes to remain in or return to the competitive world of work. Some breathe a sigh of relief when they no longer have to put in 40 hours a week to win a paycheck. Some women do have dependency needs. They want a man to take care of them. In return, they derive pleasure from the achievements of their husbands as well as the progress of their children. They do not wish to be working wives.

No one has been able to categorize what ground rules should be invoked to judge a marriage as "good" or "excellent." No two of us are alike in desires or needs. There are even some spouses who have a masochistic need to be constantly condemned. I have counseled in situations in which the wife or husband is subjected to constant verbal abuse, yet the marriage persists. Such people have a need to yell and scream at each other. This is the exception. Few of us would want a marriage with constant discord. In the typical good marriage there are bound to be occasional disagreements; however, they are resolved in an amicable manner.

When there are children, the home should be a place in which they are happy. Occasionally one finds an apparently happy marriage in which the spouses live in complete harmony while largely ignoring the children. Such youngsters tend almost to raise themselves. Having no one to give them guidance, they find they are fending for themselves and making all of their own decisions. The parents are too busy or disinterested to do much with them. You often hear the complaint, "The Smith kids down the block have parents who really neglect them. Yet they are fine children, and they seem to be doing great. I worry and fuss over my brood, and they are not doing any better. Maybe the right way is to be more casual. Perhaps I am overly protective." Upon closer examination, however, you may discover that the children of disinterested parents are not content: "I wish I could talk to my folks. They are always too busy. Mom has her bridge games and her committee work. Dad works all day and comes home too bushed to have much time for us. I almost feel as if I am growing up alone, even though I have parents who say that they love me. What can I do about it? I cannot seem to break through to them. I almost wish that there was some discipline. I do not know the limits of anything. Maybe I have too much freedom." Such thoughts are not likely to be expressed verbally to the parents. They are in the mind but remain unspoken.

Patience

A good marriage requires patience. Goals are not reached in an instant. Problems are not solved overnight. Even an active, satisfying sex life cannot be the whole answer to what life demands of us. A patient person can set goals and gradually work to attain them. Unfortunately, many people enter marriage not really sure of what they want to achieve. Maybe they just want to be happy. The word happiness, as we have seen, is difficult to define. Happiness may be seen as a "process." We are on the way to contentment as we strive to realize the goals that are yet to be reached. The couple that can practice patience are likely to be the most satisfied. A marriage that is merely serviceable can evolve into a good marriage if the couple are willing to take the time to work things through. Separation occurs when the patience level is exceeded. People of quick temper and flaring anger seldom possess the temperament to make a marriage last.

Patience involves both spouses. Decisions cannot be made on the spur of the moment. Sometimes it is better to wait than to act in haste. Hasty decisions get us into a great deal of trouble: "Alan cannot stop running. He never slows down. We always have to be on the go. Even on vacation, he tries to close a business deal. He carries his business with him every moment of his life. He does not know what it is to relax. When he has a few days of free time, he goes crazy. He is a workaholic. I love my husband, but I fear he is driving himself to an early grave. When I tell him to slow down and enjoy life, he gives me a rather confused stare. He is only happy when he is working on some big business deal. The children almost never see him. Their father is a top executive, and I am afraid he is a prime candidate for an ulcer. He will not go for counseling, since he says he feels fine and enjoys his life-style. Our family certainly does not lack anything in the way of material comfort, but I still cannot help being concerned. The man has no patience. He is in perpetual motion." Couples do need time to be alone together, without being rushed and harassed.

Our society makes stringent demands. There are always bills to pay and obligations to fulfill. Most of us live according to rather rigid guidelines. Where is the stability that makes society function? We may secretly envy those who can live one day at a time and not be overly worried about completing a task by a given deadline. It may be that we live too completely by the clock. As a young person you lead a structured life. In school the bell rings to signal the beginning or the end of a class. When you get into the world of work, you may find yourself punching a time clock. Promptness is a virtue. Hard work is part of the American ethic. So we push ahead, seeking a promotion. We become impatient. We want results. Sometimes we are goaded by our boss, who in turn is being pressured by his boss. There is a chain of pressure, emanating from the highest offices of a large company. Results are needed. What is the bottom line? Has the company shown a profit or a loss for the quarter?

In the marriage situation we also tend to become impatient: "When will the children finally grow up, so that we can have a few bucks to enjoy ourselves? It seems like every dollar I earn goes to pay for something the kids need. I love my children, but I must confess that there are many times when I wish they were done with college and out on their own. I would like to live a little, too. Today's kids have too much handed to them. I cannot wait for the time when they will hustle for a dollar themselves. Let them see how hard it is to make ends meet."

To Enjoy Each Day

In a good marriage it should be possible to live each day fully and to enjoy the many small pleasures of life. For many people pleasure is something that will occur when their working days are over: "When the kids are finally out of the house for good, Louise and I are going to travel. We have a long list of places to go and things to do. We aren't too happy now, but in only a few more years I will reach the magic age of sixty-five. Then I will be able to do all the things I have waited a lifetime to do." It is better to live each day to the utmost, and not to expect that happiness will come in advanced middle age. By that time, the diseases of older age may strike, so that pleasure deferred may never be truly enjoyed.

On their wedding day, couples do hope and pray that each day will be thrilling and satisfying. If they have patience and get the most out of each situation, this can be true. If they are unduly impatient to reach the goal of success, they may find they are torturing themselves and their mates in the frantic push to "make it big."

It would be fine if patience were taught to children from their earliest years. Our society is so busy being busy that life often slips by, and we do not savor the pure luxury of the very moment we are now experiencing.

Honesty

It is part of the Scout code to be truthful. Yet how difficult it is to be honest! We do not want to hurt the other person. We fear that we will lose their friendship or that they may retaliate with some biting criticism of us. Exchanges may follow that can be traumatic. "I cannot be honest with Jeanne. She really does not want to know how badly things are going with my business. She cannot accept the fact that we are in a slide. I just do not have the money to cover her expensive taste in clothing. Whenever I try to broach the subject, she walks away. She flees from reality. Ours is not an honest relationship. She lives in a dream world, in which I am Prince Charming who will always be the protector of our castle. I cannot bring her down to earth. She cannot face reality. I cannot discuss unpleasant things with her. She wants me to 'make nice,' as if I were talking to a little child who needs to be comforted. What can I do? If our marriage is to survive, I will have to be honest with her. I do not think she is capable of listening. She certainly does not know how to level with me. I have never been able to get to her true feelings. She is a great actress, always playing the role of loving wife and adoring mother. We all become part of her act. Fantasy may be all right to a point, but I have just about had it. What can I do to wake her up? If I break through her dream world, will I destroy her? Maybe the two of us need help from a marriage counselor."

Honesty does not mean brutality. It is not what you say but how you say it. You can speak honestly about what is in your heart without using a tone of criticism toward your spouse. If you are unsure, why not say so? In a good marriage each member of the family should be allowed to have their strengths and weaknesses tested. What good is accomplished if a marriage is based on shielding your mate from all unpleasantness? "I never let Arthur know the things that bother me. It would only upset him. I believe in keeping things going on an even keel. He only wants to hear good news. Besides, if we spoke honestly about our feelings, it might be injurious to his health. He has enough to contend with at the office. He doesn't bring his business troubles home with him, and I sure as heck will not share my thoughts with him. It is better this way. We can make each other happy by avoiding unpleasantness of any kind." Such an attitude makes for a one-dimensional marriage. There is no depth when we are unable to be honest. Play-acting is fine for the stage. Yet the plays that capture our attention usually deal with real persons, expressing real thoughts. The phony, superficial drama is not likely to be a success. The fascination with the daytime soap operas may be more than their escape value. It may be that we are seeking truth and enjoy confrontations (even vicarious) in which no holds are barred and people speak what is really on their minds. Again, it must be stressed that honest ideas can be expressed with a degree of diplomacy. You need not devastate someone by telling them the truth as you see it. Gentle persuasion may be more effective than stern moralizing and truth-telling.

A Sense of Humor

Everyone enjoys a good laugh. Laughter can often ease a tense situation. Life is grim enough without making it more so. Part of the success of marriage is the ability to joke and laugh and give and receive pleasure. Gentle, loving teasing has its place. The ability to laugh at ourselves and our own mistakes is often the tonic that relieves a potentially difficult situation. To be human is to see the ridiculous side of things. Much that is wrong can be handled with a sense of the funny. The good-humored person can withstand the blows that life has to offer. There is usually a comic side to even the most tragic situations. Laughter is a great way to release feelings.

In the family, are we able to laugh at the antics of a small child who knocks over a glass of milk at the table? Or do we end up screaming and beating the youngster? One can get out of patience with children; that is only human. Yet to survive one has to be able to see the funny side of life. Some gentle kidding can relieve the most tense situations.

While it may be apocryphal, I once heard a story about a wedding in a large New York catering hall. Several weddings were going on at the same time. In one of the chapels the groom went forward to join his bride. As they met half way down the aisle, they looked at each other in disbelief. It was the wrong bride! The girl composed herself, realized the mistake, and continued down the aisle and out the side door. A few minutes later the correct bride appeared. At this point, the best man said to the rabbi in a loud stage-whisper: "Hey, this is a terrific wedding. You even get your choice of brides!"

We know that the choice of the bride and groom is made long before they march down the aisle. But if they are in good spirits, laughing and joking before the procession begins, one has the feeling that such a marriage will turn out fine. If the couple are grimly determined about the marriage, I instinctively sense trouble.

When I was in graduate school, someone asked one of the professors, "What will we remember after we graduate?" The professor replied with a twinkle in his eyes, "The things you will remember are not the material that is formally taught in the classes. What you will remember are the funny incidents that happen in class or in the dormitory." How correct that teacher was! Life is the greatest teacher, and the foibles of the human situation are often deeply imprinted upon the mind. In a good marriage, if you can come "smiling through" a crisis, you are on the way toward happiness. When we think about it, to be happy often means to be able to smile or to laugh. A bride and groom who laugh and dance and enjoy their wedding party are likely to carry that spirit into their future relationship.

A good marriage requires a bit of happy, humorous relaxation as an essential ingredient in the prescription for a joyous union.

Timing

A good marriage contains a sense of timing. There are occasions when a family member needs to be alone. Constant togetherness is not healthy. A couple that live in an efficiency apartment will find that they frequently get on each other's nerves. It is not a sign of a lack of love to want to be by yourself for a while, and there are certainly times when it is important for you to be with your mate. Timing is easy for some and difficult for others. There are persons who barge right in and upset the balance of things. There are people who do not sense when they should be either starting or breaking off a conversation. In sports a sense of timing is essential for success. The right move at the right moment on the tennis court can bring victory. The golfer who finds that his game is on target has a finely tuned sense of timing in his swing.

In marriage there is also a need for timing. If you feel that your partner is in a receptive mood, that might be the exact moment to bring up a troubling problem.

The book of Ecclesiastes says there is a time to speak and a time to keep silent. When we visit a house of mourning, it may be best to say very little. On the other hand, if someone is weeping hysterically, we cannot stand idly by. A hand on the shoulder and a few words may give reassurance and calm the person so that she can function. The proper word may save a deteriorating social situation. A good hostess may skillfully bring people together with just the right remark or question. If you are aware of timing, you can find that moment when it may be helpful to sit down and speak with your child. Children lack this skill. They tend to be very direct, unaware that they may offend our sensibilities. They often blurt out whatever is on their minds. We laugh and excuse them because they do not know better.

If we can respond to the needs of others at the right moment it can be satisfying in the fullest sense of the word. "John always seems to sense my moods. He knows when a kind word or a smile will perk up my spirits. I don't know how he does it. I guess it is a skill that some people are born with. Me, I'm too thick to sense what is needed in so many situations. It is as if he looks with an inner eye. He sees more than most people. He is so very aware. So much that goes over my head, he grasps intuitively, and he knows how to turn a phrase. His father is the same way. Maybe it's hereditary. I sure wish I could be like him."

Timing is important in a good marriage. It has to do with plans that we make and projects that we contemplate. No home is filled with laughter all the time. There is a time to laugh and a time to weep. If we know the proper time to do each, then we have a better marriage that can withstand a variety of pressures.

How You Look at It

We may very well conclude that the good marriage is one that the partners feel is satisfactory. The outside world may look upon your marriage with a skeptical eye, but if you and your family are happy what the world thinks is not important.

You may live in a modest home on the wrong side of the tracks. Your parents may make a very modest living. You may not have all the financial advantages of your friends. You may have to work while they are free to travel. If one were to list the advantages and disadvantages of your home as compared to that of a more affluent friend, it might appear that you are suffering. Yet if your home is filled with love and laughter, you are possessed of great emotional wealth. I am not advocating poverty as a way of life. I am saying that material success is not the only measure of happiness. Even as poverty can destroy a family, so can an abundance of wealth.

Your self-image is vital. If you feel good about yourself and about your family, you are a happy, well-adjusted person. If you live in a home whose members really are pleased with each other's successes while being supportive of each other in times of distress, you can rejoice in your situation.

The terms good and bad are relative. What one family considers good, another might consider to be just the opposite. It has to do with developing goals. What is a good marriage? I have tried to define some of the ingredients that are found in families that share a common feeling of respect and love. You might be able to work up a different list of criteria for the happy home. It is not difficult to describe a good marriage. Actually making a good marriage work is something quite different. No marriage is good unless all members of the family can enjoy a reasonable degree of happiness. One need not live in ecstasy to have a good marriage. Most of us will settle for a solid relationship based on mutual respect and trust. And if we like each other, there is the best chance for a mutually rewarding life experience.

A Common Life-Style

In a good marriage you should have a great deal in common with your mate. The more alike you are as to interests, enthusiasms, and ideas, the better is your chance for marital success. Opposites may attract, but they seldom remain together. In most lasting marriages you should be able to share and care about many of the same things. This commonality of interests will draw you even more closely together. If you are fairly close in age, are of the same social background, have the same religion, enjoy similar sport and recreation activities, have enthusiasm for many of the same things in art, music, and drama, you have a good chance of succeeding. There is no harm in having some divergent interests, but the more we are alike, the better it is likely to be for our marriage: "Bill and I seldom are together. He prefers to sit in front of the TV every night. He never misses a sports event on the tube. I would like to get out once in a while to a movie or a concert. We don't like the same people. He can't stand my friends, and I find his friends boring. I often wonder why we ever got married. All we have in common is the fact that we love our kids. When they grow up, we will have nothing. We have little enough to talk about even now." Such a remark, from a woman in deep despair, is indicative of the importance of having a great deal in common with your spouse.

Maturing Together

How can we measure maturity? Some people never really grow up. Others are born with an innate sense of maturity. They know what is important. Early in life they develop their goals. They know what they want and set about getting it. Why are some mature and others immature? It could be a matter of sociology, of how we are raised in relationship to others. Or it might have to do with the skill with which we are given responsibility in our formative years. Whatever the reason, some seem to have it, and others do not.

In a good marriage the couple grow more mature as the years go by. The longer they are together, the better they are able to adjust to emerging life situations. They can weather any storm, since they have weathered other storms in the past. Each year they accumulate more and more knowledge about themselves and about their mates and families. They possess the wisdom that comes with a mature and sane attitude toward life. They realize that it takes time to work through problems. They are not in any great rush. They can move with deliberate speed when necessary. On the other hand, they know when to slow down and rest. There is a certain rhythm about their lives that their friends tend to envy. They know where they are going, since they know where they have been. Each crisis is faced as best as possible. They know their limits and can work within them. Because they respect each other, they consult each other on major decisions. As mature human beings, they make allowances for the faults of others. Not expecting perfection from their children, they do not demand perfection of themselves or of their mates. Their house is calm because they have an idea where they are heading. They are not given to the infantile behavior of threats and abuse. They do not threaten to withhold love in order to win a point or get their way. In most cases they can talk things out without shouting and angry recriminations. They are able to face disappointment and accept success with equanimity. Because they love each other, they know that often in life we have to settle for less than we had desired. They have a sixth sense about each other's feelings and can act accordingly. When necessary, they can act as one. Their unity on important matters gives them strength. In short, they are mature persons who are not afraid of tomorrow. They take their marriage vows seriously and have every intention of living together for a lifetime; and they live together not just as an escape from loneliness, but because they are in love and are good friends. All of this is involved in the maturing process of a good marriage. When these ingredients mesh in harmony, you have an excellent relationship. And even if there is some disfunction, it can be accepted with a measure of good humor. After all, who is perfect?

Thought Questions

1. How important is love in a marriage? Can a marriage exist without it? What about a sense of humor?
2. How would you describe an ideal marriage? Have you ever seen such a thing? Is it possible?
3. Why do we say there are no guarantees in marriage?
4. How important is it to have faith in your marriage partner?
5. Do you think it is important to have many things in common with your mate—or is life more exciting if you are very different from your spouse?
6. How honest can you really be with someone you love?

CHAPTER IV

Effects of Divorce

The sociology class I was teaching had ended. During the hour we had been discussing marriage and divorce. One of the students lingered. She looked at me and said, "Dr. Raab, I do not intend to rush into marriage. I am not even sure marriage is for me." "Why," I asked, "do you feel that way?" "My parents were divorced. Each has remarried. My mother has been married and divorced twice. I want to be very sure that when I marry it will be forever." Another student chimed in, "Mary, you have become cynical. Marriage is important. I look forward to it, and I expect to make it last. Sure, there are dangers. But I really do want to get married someday."

Effects on the Children

If your parents have divorced, you will have to make many adjustments. The ideal situation is to have two parents. Boys and girls need both male and female figures with whom to identify. A divorced mother will say, "I find I can cope with my daughter. We have lots in common. But at the same time a young girl needs a father. We sure could use a male around the house." A son who is in a single-parent family may declare, "Mom is great. Sure, she gets nervous and screams sometimes. It is good to have a mother, but it would be great to have a father who could take you to a ballgame once in a while." Current statistics indicate that in 13 percent of American households the children are being raised by one parent. This means that in 1.3 homes out of every 10 homes a parent is absent. In 67 percent of American families the children have their two natural parents. In 20 percent there are two parents, but one is not the natural parent.

What does this mean for the child? It requires a special degree of maturity for a child to accept the fact that he or she is being raised by one parent. It is not unusual for a child to deny to friends that he or she is fatherless or motherless. He or she may say, "I don't want to be teased or considered different from the other kids just because I don't have a mother." When a parent has died, the

41

trauma and pain can linger for a long time. If you lose a parent when you are a young adolescent, the loss is especially painful. Your mother or father is forced to assume a double role. This can be further complicated when a parent begins to date again. Some young children question each date with the words, "Are you going to be my new father (or mother)?" Children are often more open and honest than adults. They want a complete household. The American way of life almost demands two partners.

Children may become unreasonable or abusive to a new spouse who enters the picture. To the child, this is not the real mother or father. The new parent has a difficult task to restore wholeness to the fragmented family structure. What are some further effects of divorce on the child?

A Sense of Loss

Nature abhors a vacuum. The empty space created by divorce invariably produces role strain. Some have termed divorce a "living death." The spouse is absent but not completely gone. The child can be filled with pain, feeling that he somehow was the cause of the divorce. Children may have heard parents quarreling before the separation. They may even hear nasty words such as, "You care more about the children than about me."

In an earlier age, marriages were preserved for the sake of the children; divorce was not a valid alternative. In such a setting, couples stayed together in very "bad" marriages. But they were marriages, and the outer forms remained. Some were "brother-sister" arrangements, where the partners had not lived together as husband and wife for many years. Love was long gone. In such situations, what little satisfaction was left in the marriage was based upon each parent's "living through" the children. It was not unusual for such parents to seek to ally the child to themselves, to support them, in their grievances against the other spouse.

When divorce becomes a reality, a truly deep sense of loss can set in. If dad leaves, mom may be forced to go out and find a job. The child may come home to an empty house after school.

More drastic adjustments can occur. The father leaves, and the wife does not receive sufficient support to maintain the home. In such a case, the mother may be forced to move to smaller quarters in another part of town, and the child finds he must make new friends. He resents the major upsets that afflict his life. He may now see his father only on weekends. He may hear nasty comments from one or both of his parents about the other. Even if the parents have declared a truce and have mutually decided not to poison the child's mind against the other, the youngster may grasp just from the tone of voice how one parent feels about the other. The affect, that is, the emotional quality of the voice, can have a lasting effect on the child. If a mother says, "Oh, your father has enough money to buy you toys but he cannot send us enough for the rent," the child quickly catches the drift of the mother's feelings and attitudes. On the other hand, if the father on visiting day complains that the mother threw him out of the house and he now is forced to live in a dingy one-room apartment, there is bound to be a negative effect on his child.

The child of divorced parents may begin to do poorly in school. His emotional roots have been shaken to the core. He may become despondent and say, "When will dad (or mother) come back?" Loss can be accompanied by wishing that things were otherwise. If the wife says, "Your father left us," the child can turn against his dad. More often than not, the child is used as a weapon as the parents act out their sense of rage and outrage at the other. Divorce is seldom pleasant and smoothly accomplished. One looks in vain for the "good divorce."

In one of my sociology classes, the students were discussing the fact that it is better to divorce than to live in a home where there is constant quarreling, screaming, and tension. As the discussion ebbed, one student remarked, "It is easy for you to talk. We had a divorce in our family a few years ago. I was able to take it, because I was older. My younger brother and sister never fully recovered from it. I feel that it is better to hold the family together, even if there is a lot of dissension. I would prefer a bad marriage to a good divorce." One student confessed -

This view is sometimes held, but it is not the majority opinion today. Personal happiness is stressed in our society. Psychology *modern view* teaches that if the parents are not happy, the children cannot be happy. It takes loving parents to create a loving, caring home atmosphere. When love dies, it is better to divorce. It is usually believed that one can be happier when the quarreling stops. A woman said, "I was really afraid that divorce would wreck our sons. Yet now that he is out of the house, things are delightfully calm. The kids are very helpful. They both pitch in and do many things that their dad was supposed to do. And they do see him on weekends. At first it was difficult. The kids felt the loss even more than I did. Now it is much better. I find myself much happier. I don't have the hassles, quarrels, arguments, and fights. I have had to assume more responsibility. I have learned to balance a checkbook. My house is not cleaned as often as before, since I had to get a job. But my kids are happy because I am happy. Divorce is not the best arrangement. At night, when the kids are asleep, it would be nice to have a man in the house. But I can live with those pangs of loneliness and occasional guilt feelings. I have had my consciousness raised. I am more aware of me and who I am. I only hope my children understand."

Parents do hope that the kids understand. They can never be sure. Children prefer the predictable and the familiar. Their world of serenity is breached by divorce. They are often forced to choose sides or to comfort one or the other parent. They become hostage to the residue of rage that persists in the aftermath of divorce. They may have been summoned to court to be asked which parent they wished to live with. It is seldom an easy decision, whatever the age of the child, and it has been noted that adolescence can be the most damaging time. Just when the child needs the image of both parents in his or her life, they are not there. However, because of the sheer number of one-parent families, there is bound to be developing a subculture of the divorced family. As a child, you discover you are not alone. It may be that many in your classroom have divorced parents. Misery may not love company, but it can be of some comfort to know that others are going through a similar adjustment.

Depression

It is not unusual for persons to become depressed when divorce takes place. You may notice that a classmate has become irritable, and upon inquiry you may discover that he or she has "trouble" at home. Divorce can cause extreme fluctuations of behavior. A happy child suddenly becomes troubled. What can you do in such a situation? If a friend's parents are going through a separation you can be available as a good listener, and you should make allowances for the irritability. When a divorce occurs, at an unconscious level a child may have the feeling that he or she is somehow responsible. You can be reassuring and helpful when you are there to comfort him. You do not necessarily have to say anything. Just being around is often enough. Your friend may feel somewhat disconnected from the real world. His stable home is torn apart. He may carry the scars with him as he goes about his daily tasks. Make allowances for irrational behavior. He may not have complete control over his feelings and emotions.

If divorce occurs in your own family, what can you do if depression sets in? Your mother or father may send you to a psychologist for help. There is no disgrace in this. Sometimes you cannot express your feelings to your parents. They are too close to the situation, and they have a lot on their minds. You could need a stranger who is trained to listen and to help. You may want to see your clergyperson. Many of the clergy have received special help in counseling families who divorce. If you have always been close to your priest, minister, or rabbi, it would be well to see him or her. Divorce can bring about unusual strains and difficulties. You may be going through a period of extreme confusion. The clergy can help you bring your value system into balance.

Because a person is divorced, does that make him or her a "bad" person? Most clergypersons would say that the evil is not in the person. The difficulty is in the situation. Two very fine persons may marry and then discover that they are not compatible. If a couple are drastically different in their outlook on life, trouble seems certain to arise in their marriage. Perhaps they have different ideas about authority, about how to raise children, about how "neat" or "messy" the house should be. They may quarrel about how to spend leisure time. These differences do not make them evil or terrible. They merely show that husband and wife have different ways of looking at life and of finding satisfaction in day-to-day experiences. Had they married someone else, they might have been much happier.

The law in some states now makes allowances for "no fault" divorce. Society is coming to see that blaming one or the other person for the failure of a marriage is not the best way to approach the problem. Mates are often selected on the basis of strong physical attraction; but after a few years of marriage the attraction diminishes and the faults in the mate begin to come to the fore. What was cute in courtship becomes annoying when lived with under the same roof. Divorce is seldom caused by one act. It is usually the accumulation of many hurts and disappointments that brings the couple to the point where they determine to end the relationship. The actual break can take a child by surprise, and the shock can bring on depression. Events have got out of control. Angry shouting is replaced by sullen silence, now that dad (or mom) has left. Even a bad marriage has a certain rhythm or regularity to it. Children get used to the shouting and screaming and may think of it as normal. But with silence comes readjustment. A youngster may not cope too well. Parents are our authority figures and early role models. Suddenly, one parent is gone. The pain can lead to tension and confusion.

If you went through a divorce in your family in your pre-teens, you could have been deeply affected by it. The family is the setting in which we spend a good part of our lives. We are influenced by our parents' ideas and values even if we occasionally rebel against them. Our parents maintain a psychological hold on us for our entire lives. This does not mean that the family is evil. Attempts by some societies to break up the family structure have failed. People need to be part of a nuclear or extended group. If we are alone too much with our thoughts, we can become depressed. Life requires acting and doing. The best cure for the blues may well be to throw oneself into one's work or schooling with renewed vigor.

It is important to recognize that if you become depressed it is not likely to last forever. Depression tends to come and go. Time can bring healing if you can motivate yourself to be busy with worthwhile projects. It is necessary to fight inertia. Depression can immobilize one, and dark thoughts may enter the mind. It may be necessary to obtain professional help from someone trained in mental guidance. This does not mean that you are "crazy." All it means is that you need someone to talk to who can listen and give suggestions and guidance. When in trouble, we need others more than ever. If you feel depressed during a period of family trauma, you should be aware that it is a normal reaction. The body and mind must react, even though we wish they would not. How we feel physically is related to our mental state.

Dwelling on the Past

There is danger in concentrating too much on what happened in the past. It is natural to have a feeling of nostalgia for happier days, but we cannot bring back yesterday. Mom and dad may have loved each other several years ago. They do not love each other now. They have decided that divorce would be best for them and the children. No matter how much we might wish it could be otherwise, the reality of the situation is paramount. Part of our bodily defense is "denial." We are saying, in effect, that this new event did not happen. At a conscious level we are aware that divorce is taking place, but in our unconscious a mechanism is triggered that says, "If I admit that this is true, I will be miserable, so I will pretend that it never occurred." It is safer to live in a fantasy world where all is peaceful. Some persons retreat into such a world. In extreme cases, they lose all touch with the real world and its problems. Some denial may be helpful, as the body adjusts to pain; continued too long, it can cause damage. It is a mark of immaturity to live in the past. It may seem more comfortable and manageable, but it is seldom a healthy state.

Highs and Lows

As a result of the trauma of divorce, you may feel great one day and have the blues the next. These highs and lows occur without your having any control over them. Even under the best of circumstances, it is hard to understand why some days we feel fine and other days we feel irritable. Is it because of body chemistry or the cycles of the moon? Are we irritable because past hurts bubble up to the surface and trouble us? No one seems to have a satisfactory answer. On a cloudy day you may feel like singing, and on a sunny day you suddenly feel very down. It helps if you can, in effect, stand back from yourself and say, "Well, today I really don't feel great. I don't know why, but I'm sure it will pass." If you can develop such a mental attitude, it can help you to cope with what is impinging on your world.

It is certain that for most of us the days of depression do pass and we feel better. Life operates on alternating currents. Some days are great, others are just tolerable, and some are downright miserable. Rather than seeking answers, it may be necessary to float with the tide. One strategy is to warn others by saying, "I don't know why, but I am very angry today. So please stay out of my way, and please forgive me if I say nasty things. I am just not myself." If you can give such clear signals, people will understand. And if you are going through a divorce in the family, they will be especially sympathetic to your concerns and feelings.

Taking Sides

It is not unusual for a child to assume that a divorce is the fault of the parent who leaves the house. The very act of packing up and going away gives the impression of desertion.

In fact, the departure may have been provoked by the mate. Sometimes a person is put into such an untenable situation that he or she simply must leave, because to stay becomes unbearable. From a legal point of view, the partner who leaves may find himself or herself in a difficult situation. Blame is easier to level against the one who goes away. And, as a child, no matter how you may feel about mom or dad, you may well gravitate toward the one who stayed and cared for you. This is a natural reaction. The young depend on adults for their welfare. The absent father or mother can have trouble convincing the child that he or she is not at fault. "But you left us alone to fend for ourselves. When we needed you, you were gone. Don't think that because you send us a few dollars

you are a good person. You cannot buy our affection with money."
Thus, even though the absent parent is paying alimony and child
support, the fact that he is not physically present may negate his
good intentions and actions. In life, it is difficult to remain neutral.
Sometimes the child begins by blaming the absent parent and later
gravitates toward him. There is no pattern to the way emotions and
feelings express themselves. The absent partner who visits occasionally and bestows much love may become the favorite. The resi-
dent parent who complains constantly can in time be seen as the
villain.

It is vital for parents not to force the child to favor one or the
other. Criticism of the opposite spouse only exacerbates a difficult
situation. If the parents can indicate that both of them are on the
side of the child, and not choosing sides against each other, a much
better result can be achieved. A child may think, "I wish that both
my parents were at home. Since they are not, it would be great if
they would not down each other." Few points are scored by criticism of your opposite number. The child must recognize that mis-
understandings do arise and that a parent may—from a sense of
anger, hurt, and guilt—place blame upon the spouse. We are all
subject to moments of frustration.

If you are in a home where divorce is occurring, it is important to
understand some of the dynamics of the situation. Words can be
spoken in anger. It is difficult to discount what has been said. Often
parents wish they had not said certain things or acted in an unpleasant way, but spoken words cannot be "unspoken." If you can
understand that charges and recriminations that grow out of anger
are not the product of reasoned thought, it might help you to sort
out fact from fiction.

It should also be noted that some parents do deliberately manipu-
late the child, and he or she becomes a pawn in the struggle for
parental affection. A child can also be used as a spy; after a visit
with dad, a mother may ask, "What did he say about me?" This puts
the child on the spot, and makes for further problems.

Legal Effects

Once, while dining with friends at their home, the phone rang.
Our host answered it. When he returned to the table he said to me,
"Bob, I wish Harold had called you first. He was screaming that
his wife had locked him out of his house. He called me to find out
what his legal rights are." My lawyer friend sighed. "Society would
be better off if partners to troubled marriages would see their clergy-

persons before rushing to their attorneys." The scene is typical of the reactions of many when divorce is imminent. A man once told me, "I was truly amazed. I thought that we had a reasonably good marriage. Now I find out that for months my wife has been huddling with an attorney to find out how she can grab the house, car, and children when she sues me for divorce." I asked if he and his wife had talked about marriage counseling. Yes, he said, they had considered it but had decided it would not do much good. They felt they could work things out between them. The result was that they ended up in divorce court. This is not to say that family therapy would have saved their marriage. But, far too often, persons do not exhaust all possible remedies before going to an attorney. And as soon as legal proceedings begin, the partners are placed in an adversary relationship. Each has his or her own lawyer. Each is urged to be sure that all of his or her rights are protected. Squabbles over who is to get the house, the car, the boat, the condominium can quickly arise. It is not unusual for the children to become pawns in the power struggle between the parents.

Legal matters may drag on for months or years. The longer the delay, the greater the bitterness and frustration. If the frustration is severe enough, one parent or the other may "kidnap" the child and flee to another state. When this occurs, jurisdictional disputes arise and drag on and on. The costs mount as the partners duel with each other. Thus, there can be financial as well as emotional debilitation in divorce proceedings. The law seeks to be fair and to protect all who are involved in the divorce, yet the partner with the more skilled lawyer may win the day in court.

Bitterness can persist long after the divorce is final. One partner may feel that he was cheated in the settlement. The blame may be leveled at his lawyer, who he felt did not try hard enough. A husband laments: "I paid my lawyer $1,000 to take my case. I had the goods on my wife. She had committed adultery. Still, her lawyer pushed hard to get alimony from me, and my lawyer urged me to give her a generous settlement. What kind of legal advice is that? I borrowed money from friends to hire what I thought was the best legal counsel. Now I will have to borrow more money to get a better lawyer. Whom can I complain to? My wife ran away with the stocks and bonds, and she emptied our checking and savings accounts. My present attorney says there is little I can do about it. It just doesn't seem fair that she can get away with what she has done. When she cleaned me out and left, I thought maybe she was mentally ill. Now I wonder if maybe I am the sick one? What can I do?"

The offended partner can feel alone, defenseless, and deserted. His friends quickly tire of hearing his tale of woe. They may even suspect that he is exaggerating. The divorced man or woman may find himself or herself quite alone. Friends suddenly disappear. People often feel that they must choose sides. Shall I retain my friendship with the husband or the wife? Few are able to be friendly with both. It is necessary to ventilate anger, but anger cannot sustain one forever, and it may drive away persons who otherwise might rally round.

Second Thoughts

When divorce occurs, a person may feel that he or she is not worth very much. Divorce is often viewed as personal failure. A partner may believe that she was not loving enough or considerate enough, or perhaps she did not encourage her mate sufficiently. Divorce can bring on some stock-taking. Did I let myself go in appearance? I look in the mirror, and I don't see the slim, attractive, neatly groomed girl that my husband adored. The husband may also do some self-analysis. He may discover that he was often irritable and unreasonable. Second thoughts are bound to come to mind. Did I do the right thing? It seemed so right for me to leave. We had absolutely nothing in common outside of the kids. We loved them, but we really didn't enjoy each other's company. I would put in extra hours at the office to avoid the hassles and arguments at home. She spent more and more time with her friends. When I did want to talk to her, she always had someplace to go or a friend to call. I became the disciplinarian of the kids, but I was not really a husband and father. Yet, with all this, we did have some good times. It would be painful for me to look at our wedding album. We looked so happy that day. Our whole future was before us. I had very little money, but she didn't seem to care. We were so excited about the life we would share. Now, ten years later, everything has fallen apart. Well, we are divorced. Here I am, living in my own small apartment. There are times when I almost miss the arguments. How can you fight with a TV set? And she has custody of the kids. She is bound to have more of their love. I feel so lost and so alone.

The foregoing are thoughts that can go through the mind. If they persist, and if the second thoughts become first thoughts, the couple may seek reconciliation. But once a divorce decree has been issued, few remarry the former spouse. The emotional and legal barriers have become so formidable that no matter how much they may regret their actions, it becomes very difficult to return. Too much anger, bitterness, and mistrust remain. Too much may have been said.

The husband now finds that the singles bars are not his style. He feels awkward about dating. He may have little money left to live on each month, once he has made his alimony and child-support payments. The wife may feel chained to the house if the children are small. She may not have enough money to hire help so that she can go out and work. Or she may find that she is not employable. She may discover that she has to go back to college to prepare herself for a job. If this is necessary, who will take care of the kids? She can suffer a loss of self-esteem, feeling that the divorce was really her fault. Maybe she did neglect her husband and place the children first. Perhaps she was not responsive enough, or comforting enough, when he turned to her. Maybe she mocked him for his failures instead of supporting him in times of trouble and stress at his job. Self-blame and doubt can lead to second thoughts. As a divorced woman, the world is not her oyster. Her married friends may shy away from her, feeling that she may try to entice their husbands. She may feel that everyone is blaming her for the divorce. Her children may be mocked and questioned by their peers. Children are not always kind. How can a child of divorce respond when a friend asks, "Why did your father move away?" The child may not know. All she knows is that daddy is gone and only visits on Sundays.

Parents can have trouble coping with their own feelings, as well as the feelings of their children. What can a parent do? What rules are to be followed? Friends and books give conflicting advice. Some authors speak of divorce as liberating and exhilarating. Others stress the evil and trauma of divorce, urging couples to stay together almost at all costs. They declare, "A bad marriage is better than a good divorce." These words may have been spoken by friends. The divorced person may even have said them herself. So-called "wise sayings" are not helpful when reality intrudes and the marriage is dissolved. There is an abundance of books on the market to advise the divorced, the remarried, and those contemplating divorce. The confused person does not know whom to believe or to trust.

New Resolutions?

The partners may resolve to try to put the past behind them and move forward. Each may discover that anger and hatred solve nothing. One can cry, scream, complain, and wail only so long. When this stage is reached, the person may look around and decide to rebuild his life. He may say, "What is the use of recrimination and anger over what Mary said. I now must become a whole person again. I cannot change her, and she obviously could not change me. Our ideas and attitudes toward the kids, politics, toward what was important—all of these were miles apart. I could not make her over into my image of the ideal wife and mother. She just could not alter her ways. I should have been aware of this before we got married, but then we were both on our best behavior. Even when we lived together for two years before the marriage, it was us against the world. We were so proud of being liberated. We were having a great adventure and not a marriage. We could shock people by our arrangement. We shared in standing firm against the world. Once we got married, everything changed. We suddenly saw that we truly had very little in common. Every time the marriage seemed to be coming apart, we had a child. Now, after the third child, we can see that it will never work. Why raise kids in a home where there is no peace? We fight, argue, and agree on practically nothing. Now we are divorcing. I will have to build a life for myself. Mary will have to set her priorities straight, too. I cannot totally blame her, although I really do feel that she had no deep feelings for me or what bothered me. Sure, I did some foolish things, but she provoked me. She always gave me the feeling that she had done me a favor by agreeing to our marriage. She always felt that she came from a much higher-class family. Her parents never said it, but by their actions I knew that they never felt I was good enough for their daughter. I could never overcome their opposition. When the chips were down, I felt she sided with her parents. We did not have a marriage. We had a relationship, whatever that means. All the fun went out of our lives. So I have resolved, once the divorce is completed, to pick up the pieces of my life and live one day at a time until I can sort out my emotions."

Mary may well have thought, "I, too, will have to reassess who I am and where I am going. I will have to rear these three kids. John was right. We thought having babies could bring us together. I had been raised by parents who said that even a bad bargain had to be honored. My folks were supportive when the divorce proceedings began. They saw, more clearly than I, what was happening in our home. Yes, my parents never really approved of John. They were shocked when we lived together for two years before the marriage. They are rather snobbish, and I know they always felt I could marry better. What can I do now? I suppose I will just have to do the best I can. At nights I often cry. It was good having a man in the house, even a man who had stopped loving me. It can be very lonely with just the children to talk to, and I can't tell them how I really feel. I guess I will join one of those therapy groups for divorced persons. Maybe misery loves company. And, who knows, maybe I will meet someone who is more like me. At the moment, my life is fragmented. As we move toward the final papers, I feel deeply hurt and abused. I can't help feeling that John is getting the better of the deal. He is out, free, and can move around at will. I am saddled with the kids. Sure, I love them, but they do tie me down to the house. I hope that not all my friends will stop calling. Right now I am getting a lot of sympathy and advice, but things will probably change once the divorce is final. I am lucky that my parents are so understanding. I do have their shoulders to cry on when things get really tough. I hope I don't do anything crazy or stupid. It is not going to be easy without a husband. But then, it was not easy having him at home, either. How can you live with someone when they say they don't love you and don't share any of your interests or concerns? I used to think that you kept a marriage together for the sake of the kids. Well, now I feel that for the sake of the kids it is better that we go our separate ways. I do have some second thoughts. We did have some great moments. But, on reflection, I realize that they all occurred before we got married. Maybe if we had never married, but continued to live together, we would have remained happy. Well, I am still young and strong, and my health is good. My parents tell me to count my blessings and start making plans for the future. Second thoughts are certainly no help. It is too late for a reconciliation. Neither of us wanted to go for marriage counseling. Maybe we were wrong, but it's too late now. Perhaps with a fresh start, things will be better. At least the noise level is lower. My kids actually seem happier with John gone. They have been a comfort to me. I wonder what they think of me? Have I failed them? It is troubling to know that you are getting a divorce. It sounds so final. It reminds you of death. But maybe it is more like a living death, since your husband will be gone and not really gone. The kids will see him regularly. I hope it does not tear them apart. For that matter, I hope I can take it."

Mary sees divorce almost as a kind of punishment. Yet sociologists and psychologists generally agree that in divorce both partners share in the fault. It can be added that maybe it is the "situation" that is wrong. Divorce does not mean that one partner is good and the other is bad. They simply are not compatible. With other mates, they might be very happy. Or they may be in that category of persons for whom marriage is not the answer. Some people are happiest living alone.

Effects on Society

Social mores impact upon our lives. We connect with others and relate to them within a social framework. Our value system is not divorced from our family system. No matter how we may battle and argue with our parents (even as they argued with our grand-parents), we do know that man is a social animal. Sociologists are convinced that most of what we do in life grows out of interpersonal relationships. Even though we may employ "differentiation," a tech-nique of going in and out of a family situation, we never fully distance ourselves from our families. When we leave our family of orientation (the family we are born into) and form our family of procreation (our new nuclear group), the history, traditions, attitudes, and feelings of those who preceded us are somehow in-ternalized into our unconscious. One is never a wholly "free" person. Those who are involved in primary (that is, intense, close) relation-ships with us are bound to influence our emotions, feelings, atti-tudes, and actions.

One may argue to what extent society creates a climate of thought and belief. We cannot separate ourselves from the culture. No couple emerge free and unfettered from the marriage ceremony. Even the ceremony itself has much social input. Parents are in-volved in wedding plans and usually in wedding costs. In some cases, a young man may borrow money from his parents to buy his girl a ring. The groom may be employed by his father. The couple may need financial help to get started. Parents may give expensive gifts, such as cars or honeymoon trips. Each time the couple accept a gift, it creates obligations. If one family is more generous to the couple than the other, it can be a source of friction. In anger, the bride may say, "Well, my folks paid for the big wedding. What did your folks do?" To which the groom may re-spond, "Well, my parents brought me into the world to support you, so they obviously did something right!"

Do Your Own Thing

In the 1960's the phrase "Do your own thing" began to be heard with increasing frequency. It was an echo of the emerging woman's rights movement. It resounded through the ranks of the young as they marched and protested against the Vietnam War. It had its antecedents in the 1950's, with the beginnings of the push for civil rights for blacks and other oppressed minorities. The phrase became a rallying cry and slogan for young people who had begun to remove themselves from their parents. The needs of the individual came first. If I am not happy, I cannot make others happy. Until I am at peace with myself, I cannot be at peace with the world. To accomplish this, I must find myself and better understand who I am now. The "do your own thing" philosophy is very now-oriented. It depends more on feelings and emotions than on intellectual and cognitive considerations. We are what we feel we are, and not what we have been taught to be. Therefore, if I do my own thing I will find fulfillment. Earlier generations called such a view selfish and insular. Many of today's generation would say that the "hang-ups" of the past are what hold us back. We are too tied to our families and their cultural values. Only in breaking loose can we rediscover our true self and inner being.

Such a philosophy can be helpful to the timid and the shy, who are unable to be assertive. There are people who so completely devote their lives to the service of others that they have no life of their own. To be completely other-directed contains seeds of danger, even as being completely self-directed can cut one off from reality.

The danger emerges when a do-your-own-thing society has to cope with the very real problems that arise in a divorce. What happens to my sense of responsibility for my children if I am concerned only about my own happiness? Do I, as a person, have a duty to my family? If I have helped to bring children into the world, at what point do I have the right to abandon them to someone else because I am displeased with my mate or with myself. Our times are very "feeling"-oriented. We are told by some psychologists to do our own thing, even if it causes pain to others, because then— eventually—we will be happier and more mature adults. It has become less fashionable to think about the feelings of the children. How much psychological damage is being done to them? How will they survive the trauma and stress of even a "good" divorce that follows a "bad" marriage.

The complete narcissist can never be satisfied. If I am totally "me"-oriented, then what pleases me today may well repel me tomorrow. Relationships become fragile, and persons are discarded rather easily. The in-laws are often at a loss as to what to do when a couple are about to break up. Should they interfere? Psychologists urge us to be cautious and not interfere. We should let the couple "work things out." In effect, society stands idly as the endangered marriage drifts toward the rocks of destruction and divorce. Often distraught in-laws cry aloud to me, "Dr. Raab, what can I do? What should I do? I know my daughter is unhappy with her husband. She cries on my shoulder constantly. She has lost weight and is irritable. She is always fighting with her husband and screaming at the children. She looks terrible. She wants me to tell her what to do, but what can I tell her? She is a grown woman, yet she is also my child. I brought her into the world. We love our adorable grandchildren. They will be the victims. What can we do?"

The cry is echoed at many levels. Parents want to be helpful but feel they are helpless. A distraught father speaks to me: "What can I do for my daughter? We love her. She made a bad marriage, and now she has two children, and they are living on welfare. Her ex-husband never could make a living, so we support her. Now she is pregnant by a man who has no intention of marrying her. She refuses to consider having an abortion despite our urging. We see this wonderful daughter of ours sinking deeper and deeper into despair. When she was younger, she was so beautiful and full of life, hope, and promise. Today she just does not care. She let herself get heavy, she dresses in a sloppy manner, and she lives on welfare in the slums. And, with all of this, instead of trying to help herself, she gets pregnant and now will have another burden to carry. How can we get her to see her mistakes before it is too late?"

Parents are frustrated. They have had enough experience in life not to want to see their children make what in their eyes are near fatal decisions. The counselor may tell them that a daughter in her late twenties is a mature woman, but it is so difficult for parents to "let go." They have a long-standing investment, both emotional and financial, in their children. American culture measures happiness in terms of achievement and status. When a child drops out of middle-class culture and is content to live on welfare, the parents feel disgraced. Part of the problem is what one's friends and neighbors will think and say. We cannot separate ourselves from society. A person may do his own thing, but it is impossible not to affect others by one's actions, be they wise or foolish. The do-your-own-thing philosophy demands that we be ourselves. Society may be more tolerant of dropouts than the persons who are affected by the immediate event.

On a reasonable, intellectual level, it should be possible to accept what our children do and the decisions or nondecisions they make. At age eighteen one is legally considered an adult, but few eighteen-year-olds in our society are independent. Many young people live at home until well into their twenties, and some are supported by parents in graduate-school programs that can last until nearly thirty. The longer we have these strong financial and emotional ties, the more we make claims upon the recipients of our largesse. If a couple are married and depend for support upon the in-laws, it is almost as if the in-laws were living with them. It is natural to resent the hand that feeds you if you are old enough to be self-supporting. Many a cloud forms over a marriage where the couple are forced to take money or ask for financial support from relatives. Marriage has enough strain and stress without this additional burden. In a divorce situation, if the rent is still being paid by the in-laws, they often feel that they are victims along with their grandchildren. There is the real fear that if they interfere they may anger their son or daughter-in-law and not be allowed to see the grandchildren. If they are the parents of the estranged husband and the wife has custody of the children, they have a legitimate concern that the mother may, in spite, deny them access to the grandchildren. Children, then, can become victims not only of their frustrated parents, but also of the pressures brought to bear by the grandparents.

Danger Signals

What causes a divorce? There can be many outward manifestations. It could be gambling, alcohol, wife-beating, or adultery. A man who gambles away his paycheck can suffer a loss of self-respect, as his family begins to turn away from him. A woman who is a "closet alcoholic" and neglects her home and children may soon find that she is abandoned by her spouse. In the do-your-own-thing age, we have less patience with the weak and the foolish. If you cannot shape up, then ship out. If you become a nuisance, you can be replaced by others who are eager to take your place. A man who is unhappy at home has little difficulty finding comfort from a secretary at the office. A wife who has tired of her husband may find others in the same frame of mind and end up cruising the singles' bars while her husband is busy at his job. The working wife may lose respect for a husband who is not as successful as she is. It is easy for her to connect with a fellow worker in her office. Available women are in demand.

When a woman discovers that her husband is unfaithful, her friends may urge her to go out and have a "good time." If one thinks in terms of a single standard of conduct (which means that both partners in the marriage have the same freedom to act), a freer sexuality results. It is no longer unusual for married women to be on the prowl, whereas in a former age it was more common for the men to be out looking for excitement. I have been told that many male commuters have an "office" wife, and the woman really does not care whether or not her "friend" is married. A woman told me, "My husband said that at his success level, all the men have mistresses and I should not be disturbed by it. He says that the other men's wives know, but they realize that a successful executive does need some time to play." It is not easy for the middle-aged wife to accept this different moral standard. She may deeply resent living with a man who spends nights and weekends away, ostensibly on business. In like manner, a man may discover that his working wife has been unfaithful, while he has observed a strict code of sexual loyalty.

It may be that society is in the process of redefining "loyalty" and "devotion." Must we think of "being faithful" to our mates in different terms? Perhaps some would redefine the word "faithful" as meaning to be "faithful to whatever mutually agreed upon standard of conduct exists between us." With such an approach one could have an open marriage, with each partner free to have "affairs" as a way to enrich life and make it more exciting, stimulating, and free.

Lasting Effects?

Every experience leaves its mark upon us. The effects of divorce should not be minimized. It touches the couple, their children, and the grandparents. Even though the divorce rate is high and continues to go higher, the American norm is the undivorced couple. Divorce brings on separation and bitterness. Even in good divorces, the estrangement can be difficult. Emotional costs must be paid. The most sophisticated bear scars. In time, the scars heal and new relationships can begin to form. Young people are bound to feel the effect, but if you can accept the idea that, in many cases, to continue to live together is worse than separation, you will find the strength and wisdom to cope.

Thought Questions

1. Why do parents worry so much about the effect of divorce on their children?
2. What is lost when couples break up?
3. Is a bad marriage preferable to a good divorce?
4. Should parents stay together for the sake of the children?
5. Why are children often forced to take sides when a divorce occurs? How does this affect the children?
6. Why is society so concerned that marriages remain stable?

CHAPTER V

Some Causes of Divorce

Sociologists, economists, and social thinkers have wrestled with the question of what really brings on divorce in our society. Some tentative answers seem to be emerging.

Mobility

Our postindustrial age brings frequent moves. To advance in business, it is often necessary to move to a new community. If one wishes to rise on the corporate or professional ladder, one must "move on." Not everyone can adjust to the constant need to seek new roots, only to discover a year or two later that one must again summon the moving vans. With one of every seven Americans moving each year, there is bound to be dislocation. Look at your neighborhood for a moment. How many neighbors do you see who were there when you moved into your home? Perhaps you yourself have newly moved into an area. Was it difficult for you to make friends in a new school? Did your parents find that people were slow to accept them? Humans are social beings. People do, indeed, need people. We do not live in a vacuum. The constant stress of mobility can put pressure on families. How many times is it fun to move and meet new people? There can be a sense of novelty about moving, but there is also fear, incipient loneliness, and the knowledge that old friends are gone and may never be seen again.

A wife says, "I could not adjust. Tom's company has moved him on the average of once every three years. I feel like an army wife. No sooner do we develop some friends when suddenly we have to pull up stakes and leave. It has been hard on the kids. I guess it is worse for them. They often cry at night. People say that kids are flexible and can adjust easily to new situations, but it is not always so. Then there is the uncertainty. We are here today. Will we be gone tomorrow? Sure, we write letters to old friends, but we will probably never see them. Our oldest child, Annie, is a senior in high school. She cannot look back on her teen years as a time of lasting friendships. To her, high school graduation means little. Her real friends are miles away. I feel for her, but what can I do? I don't want to stop Tom. He is ambitious. He assures me that soon he will be back in the home office, in a top job with the company. Tom is a go-getter. His family suffers. Lately, I have fantasized what life would be like if I just said, 'No more moves.' What would Tom do? My guess is, we would get a lawyer and file for divorce. I still love Tom, but I don't know how much longer I can take these constant dislocations. Our marriage is a shambles, even if Tom is not aware of how the kids and I feel."

The foregoing comments are not unusual. Many wives of top executives bear the scars of constantly being uprooted, and along the way many do falter and get divorced. A study in *Fortune* magazine showed that corporations are changing their attitude toward divorced men. At one time, to be divorced was a disgrace and would hinder promotion. Today, many large corporations welcome the divorced male and female, feeling that they will give their all to the company, since they will not be burdened with families that might make demands on their time and energy.

Statistics show that 20 percent of the top executives of 500 major corporations are divorced, and the number is growing. We may be reaching a stage where the desire to "meet the little woman to see if she fits the corporate image" may become a thing of the past. The new, aggressive, unencumbered divorced person emerges as a very desirable and upwardly mobile person. He or she need not agonize over spending too much time in the office or on trips. Divorce gives one greater mobility. In an ever-moving society, roots are becoming old-fashioned. International global business deals can whisk a person from one end of the earth to another. Who has time for family? Children need the attention of parents. Children cannot be taken on business trips. So the American life-style is one of "moving on," hopefully to a better opportunity and greater affluence.

Sexual Freedom

We live in a much more permissive society. Teenage pregnancies are on the rise. Yet who listens to the confused young person? The sexually permissive society is geared to a strong emphasis on what pleases the individual. I become very concerned about what makes me happy and satisfied. In an earlier age sex was confined for the most part to the marriage bed. The male might be "experienced" on his wedding night, but the bride was not to have slept with any-one else. Sex was to be part of the normal bonding of a couple, an expression of shared hopes, dreams, and excitement.

One can argue about the virtues or drawbacks of the newer, freer morality. It does, however, seem evident that our age has seen an increase in divorce even as there is a rise in premarital sex. If we can believe some of the studies, adultery is far more common than we thought it to be. If sex is just a way to ease a biological urge, the person who satisfies that urge may be seen more as an object than as a person. The Playboy philosophy looks upon girls as bunnies to be enjoyed, played with, and then discarded. To be cool means to be uninvolved, disengaged. The world is easy. Easy come and easy go. I enjoy you today, and I leave you tomorrow. Commitments are tentative. Let's try things out. Let us live together for a time and see if we are really in love. Marriage, rather than being the beginning of a relationship, is often the culmination of months or years of living together. "We had to check each other out. Neither of us were that sure. We had to be sure we enjoyed sex with each other." In the period before marriage many couples come to know each other quite well from a sexual point of view. As one young man said with a sigh, "I wonder if marriage will be much different from what Jean and I have going with each other now?"

The defenders of the so-called new morality (or is it really a throwback to an older morality) contend that sexual freedom helps couples to be more sure of a relationship before they solemnize it with the marriage vows. Statistics can be quoted on both sides of the issue. Some say that those who have lived together are better prepared for the reality of marriage. "John and I got to know each other. You cannot hide your faults when you share the same apartment. It was a small step from living together to setting the date for the wedding. We just wanted to be sure that when we got married it would last. Both of us have a lot of divorce in our families. We really are trying, at all costs, not to leap before we are as sure as we can be about our feelings for each other. Yes, we have been under pressure from our families. They wanted us to wed when we first began going together. My mother still cannot accept the idea of her daughter's living in sin. My dad is even worse. He really does not like John. Dad feels that John seduced me and is using me to have some fun, and then—when he gets tired of me—he will walk out. Dad does not seem to realize that I could get tired of John and just walk out on him, too."

It is no longer a man's world as it once was. Sometimes it is hard to make your parents understand this. A woman can "use" a guy just as often as a guy can "use" a girl. The world changes. The values of yesterday have been altered or discarded. Modernists argue that in time the new sexual freedom will bring about more stability in marriage, since the partners will be more "experienced" before they stand at the altar. If you really know the other person, you do not walk blindly up the aisle. You know what to expect. Living together is thus seen as preparation for marriage. It is a time of testing and deciding whether or not each person really wants to be married. It is a period to free oneself of sexual "hang-ups" and illusions. The media glorify "easy" sex as the new normal way. Premarital virginity becomes increasingly rare, not alone in males but also in females. Males no longer expect the bride to be a virgin on her wedding night.

There are those who argue that a freer sex ethic leads to divorce. Where, they ask, are the boundaries? Where are the rules for the couple to follow? How many acts of adultery can be tolerated before the marriage crumbles? Even in an "open marriage," are the emotions of jealousy and rage to be exorcised out of relationships? How many couples are capable of maintaining a marriage in which "swinging" becomes a way of lending new excitement to fading romance? Some will go the route of the "swingers," but this is not likely to be the pathway of the majority. Sexual fidelity is still— with all the new freedom—expected by the partners in a marriage. The bride may have lived with the groom for a number of years, but this does not mean that either one will easily and readily tolerate the other's being unfaithful.

While many segments of American society tolerate sexual freedom before marriage, once the wedding takes place the couple is bonded, and fidelity is to be the rule and infidelity the exception.

Why infidelity? One wife speaks, "I guess I was unfaithful to Morton in my mind for a long time. Then I sort of drifted into an affair. It really was not planned. Mort was busy at his job and was always tired at night. We never seemed to go anywhere. Our sex had become very perfunctory. There was no excitement. The thrill was gone. I guess I was open and ready for some new adventure. I was unfaithful. I did commit adultery. I still do, now and then. I don't think Mort knows. And, frankly, even if he did know, I wonder if it would bother him. He seems to lack the energy even to be jealous."

Sexual infidelity may be due to boredom or other aspects of unhappiness. When it occurs with frequency, there is often trouble keeping the marriage afloat. A woman says, "How long can this go on? Bill is unfaithful. I know it, and he knows I know it. He says that he could never be fully satisfied by one woman. He says his relationship to me is special, and these side-trips are just diversions. He does always, in time, come back to me. He knows how upset I am. I really don't know what to do. If I pushed him, I guess we could get a divorce. But where would I be then? I would be just another middle-aged gal, hanging around bars, looking for men. I don't want to be alone. I suppose I'll stick it out as long as I can."

Choices are not always easy to make. Children often are aware of their parents' actions. They hear much more than we suspect. Where adultery abounds, a child may feel threatened. The only world he knows seems to be on the brink of destruction. Yet what can a child do? He must wait, hope, and wonder. Children who come from unhappy homes may be averse to rushing into marriage. They have seen bitterness in their own house; why should they rush into marriage? Besides, "meaningful relationships" are quite possible to develop, since adult society is not shocked by the sight of the young living together.

Sexual attraction is vital to a good marriage. Yet many marriages function with a minimum of coitus. Not all partners are eager for sex. Wives and husbands have confessed to their therapists that sex is "not such a big deal," and they can live very nicely with a minimum of it. There are congenial marriages in which from their inception the romance was low key.

Arguments can be made both for and against the newly emerging sexual life-styles. What does seem evident is that a freer sexual morality is very much in vogue now, and, talking to young people, it seems unlikely that they will go back to the more puritan ways of past generations. Many are carried along with the new life-styles, whether or not they feel comfortable with these modes of inter-personal relationships.

Situation ethics would say that I do what I wish to do in any given situation, so long as it is not harmful to another person. Where this principle is applied in the realm of sexual conduct, it denotes a search—by trial and error—for a compatible bedmate. Such bedmates may, in time, become marital mates. Whatever one thinks of the freer sexuality, it obviously has to be dealt with. How it will affect the divorce rate of the future is anybody's guess. For the moment, freer sexuality and higher divorce rates are on parallel tracks. Can we blame the new morality for more marriages breaking up? No hard statistical evidence is available. It would appear that changing sexual mores have affected the family. The pluses and minuses are still to be fully determined and evaluated.

Dishonesty

How honest should people be with each other? Obviously, one should not tell all to one's mate. This could be very destructive.

Some people simply cannot face the truth. It is best if we can be basically honest with our mates. If we honestly say what we want, we can avoid much misunderstanding and confusion. Divorce is often precipitated because partners are not truthful. They say one thing and mean something else. Tragically, some fear to speak openly for fear of displeasing the mate. A good marriage cannot be built on fear. It must be fashioned on the bedrock of faith and honesty. The more constructively honest we are, the better are the chances of success in marriage. This does not imply that your spouse must be told everything and anything. Discretion should be exercised and expected. If you say what is honestly in your mind and heart all the time, you may become a carping critic and nag. But if you never say what is your mind, you will destroy others and eventually destroy yourself as well. We need an outlet to speak of what truly touches us. In a good marriage we can be truthful, even when the truth hurts. Not to speak may in time prove far more destructive. However, too much honesty about sexual adventures can do more harm than good.

Thought Questions

1. Why is mobility a cause of divorce? Do you think it really matters how many times a family moves?
2. Does sexual permissiveness lead to divorce? Is our society too open about sexual matters?
3. Do you think any marriage can survive if there is infidelity?
4. Is it sometimes best to be dishonest with the one you love?
5. Can too much honesty destroy a relationship?

CHAPTER VI

Friendly or Unfriendly Divorce?

It is difficult to categorize divorce. Few divorces fall into neat frames of reference. It is possible, however, to try to differentiate between the various ways in which divorce manifests itself. The following are some of the varieties that one might see.

The Friendly Divorce

Mort and Edna married when they were very young and soon had children. By the time they reached their early 30's Mort was a successful businessman. Edna was content to be a loving wife and mother, who busied herself with housework, cooking, sewing, and shopping. She built her life around Mort and the children, even as she took great pride in her culinary talents. Edna laughed at the feminists who urged women to go back to school and prepare for a career. "My husband and the children are my career. No, more than that. They are my entire life." The first ten years of marriage were happy and fulfilling. Then Edna noticed that Mort was becoming restless and irritable. Nothing she did pleased him. He began to yell and scream at the children over the most trifling matters. Finally, matters came to a boiling point. Mort asked Edna for a divorce, saying that he no longer found her interesting and that his love for her had died.

After a lengthy, tear-filled confrontation, the couple decided to go to a marriage counselor. Despite many months of counseling, Mort was still determined to obtain the divorce. They had gone through all the traditional channels of trying to save their marriage. The counselor had advised them to go away on a second honeymoon, but it did not work. They were counseled to express themselves, but this only led to outbursts of anger and remorse. Mort felt that Edna had not kept up with him. He measured his wife against the knowledgeable women he met in the business world. He came to the conclusion that life with Edna was both predictable and dull. After a year of earnest effort at trying to hold the marriage together, a peaceful divorce was arranged. In fact, the couple engaged one lawyer to handle the details for both. Edna received a handsome settlement, including possession of the house and generous alimony and child support. The children remained with Edna, and Mort was given full visitation rights. There were no recriminations and few outbursts of anger. Neither parent spoke ill of the other. When matters of sending the children to camp and later to college came up, the parents were amicable in reaching decisions. In fact, they became better friends when divorced than they had been when married. The children were upset initially by the divorce, since to them it was unexpected. Mort and Edna had avoided quarreling in front of them, so the kids were taken aback when their parents told them that divorce was imminent. While the youngsters may have had some guilt feelings about the divorce, fearing that their behavior had precipitated it, these notions were quickly dissipated in discussions with their parents. So for Morton and Edna it was in truth a friendly procedure. The children continued to see their father with their mother's full consent. Since both parents remained in the same geographic area and did not remarry quickly, the children were able to retain contact with both mother and father. Few emotional scars were sustained by the family.

Effect on the Children _of a friendly divorce_

Edna's and Mort's children continued to grow and develop in an atmosphere of love, rather than hatred. Mort was wise enough not to smother them with expensive gifts when they spent weekends and holidays with him. Edna had the wisdom not to condemn her husband for leaving the family. The children saw that their dad kept up the support payments and did not welch on his obligations. Financial decisions were seldom a cause of friction. In such a harmonious atmosphere, all members of the family were able to grow in a congenial and loving manner. Early feelings of guilt and recrimination vanished, as all members of the family came to realize that divorce was the best answer when parents fell "out" of love. When Mort did remarry a few years later, his children attended the wedding and congratulated the newlyweds. Eventually Edna married a somewhat older man who was able to win the affection and respect of her children.

Effect on the Parents

Edna and Mort were spared extreme feelings of guilt because they were essentially good people who worked hard at making the divorce as painless as possible. There were difficult moments, to be sure. Splitting a family asunder is never pleasant. But stormy scenes were kept to a minimum. The parents were able to give the children, as well as each other, a full measure of emotional support. Mort felt that the divorce was a "growing" experience for him and the family. Edna was less sure of this in the initial stages of the separation. However, as time went by and the children grew older, she decided to go to college; in the course of time she received training for a full-time job. Today she is happy and busy in her work and in making a home for her new husband and her children.

Friendly Divorces—Rare or Common?

The friendly divorce is seldom played out in the uneventful script outlined above. Former partners often speak of being on "good terms" with their ex-mates, but when you look at their faces you soon discover that the words do not match the facial expressions. My own counseling experience leads me to the conclusion that most divorces are very unfriendly. Frequently suspicion, arguments over money and visiting rights, and general lack of trust characterize them. The wounds tend to linger, and time only partially heals the hurt of separation and divorce.

Coping with a Friendly Divorce

It is certainly much easier for children to live with a situation in which parents are understanding and really try to relieve them of as much pain as they can. I am sure that a young person who is in a situation where the parting is amicable will be able to make a healthy adjustment. Some children have even said, "I see more of dad now than when he lived at home. When he was always fighting with mom, he had nothing to say to us. On weekends he would sulk around the house or disappear. Since the divorce, we know that dad will spend every Sunday with us. He actually talks to us and tries to please us. So it's really nice. Of course, we do wish he had never left the house."

The Unfriendly Divorce

Joe and Harriet had been childhood sweethearts. He was the quarterback on the high school football team; she was the cutest cheerleader. Everyone remarked that they looked great together. After high school, Joe was drafted into the army. Upon his discharge, he married Harriet. Joe enrolled in college and Harriet got a job to help support them. In time Joe finished college and went to work. Harriet never wanted to go to college. She went to secretarial school and became a very efficient secretary. When the first child arrived, Harriet said, "I hope I never have to go back to work again." For a number of years she settled in as wife and mother. But after the second child much bickering developed. Joe accused her of paying more attention to the children than to him. She began to see that Joe was very childish and self-centered. He had become jealous of the time she gave to the children. No matter what she did, she could not please her husband.

Matters finally came to a head in a quarrel over which in-laws' home to visit for Thanksgiving. After a stormy quarrel, Joe walked out of the house and spent the weekend with his parents. He found that he really did not miss Harriet and the kids. His parents' home was orderly and peaceful; it seemed a sanctuary where he could retreat from the emotional battering of his own home. He confessed to his parents that he had purposely been working late hours so as to spend as little time at home as possible. His parents were sympathetic but urged him to try again for the sake of the children. With some reluctance, Joe did return to his family and had a long talk with Harriet. They both decided to try again, to patch up their battered relationship. It simply did not work. The old quarrels and recriminations reasserted themselves, and their children became increasingly disobedient and sullen. The atmosphere was heavy with suspicion and mistrust. Then Harriet discovered that Joe had been unfaithful to her. She berated him for this, and he responded that if she had been a loving and warm wife he never would have strayed. Shaken and upset, Harriet ordered Joe out of the house. The in-laws tried to bring them together, but to no avail. Matters had gone too far. Each one retained a lawyer. They fought bitterly over the financial settlement. For long periods they spoke to each other only through their lawyers. The children soon saw that each parent blamed the other for the divorce. Harriet was outspoken in denouncing Joe as an "unfit" father. Joe, in turn, made no bones about the fact that he considered Harriet to be a cold, unfeeling woman who had destroyed both him and their marriage. The word "unfriendly" was too mild to describe the divorce. It was played out in an arena of much bitterness, anger, and accusations. When the dust finally settled, the parents were not speaking to each other. The children remained with Harriet. She spoke to Joe only through the children or other third parties. "You tell your father that we need more money," was a frequent message that she gave the children. Joe also conveyed his feelings through the children. Neither parent truly knew what the other was doing. The children were raised in an atmosphere in which they were taught to hate their father, and the father in turn tried to turn the children against the mother.

As a consequence, the children developed bitter feelings against both parents. They never could understand why there was so much hatred where before there had been love. How could my parents have brought me into the world and now be so rejecting of each other? Decisions as to camp, friends, and college were not made jointly. Harriet decided what to do in raising the children and then communicated to Joe through the children that the decision was made and he was to pay the costs. Joe became furious. His lawyer was kept busy as he threatened to curb alimony and child-support payments. Harriet retaliated by telling the children that their father was "cheap" and refused to take care of them and their needs. In such a situation, the children were confused and uncertain as to what they should do. They loved their parents, but now each parent demanded loyalty at the expense of the other. In time, the children became emotionally disturbed. Their school work suffered, and the eldest child became withdrawn. The children were sent for psychiatric help, since they had been robbed of strong family roots of confidence and love. Joe and Harriet proclaimed their love for their children, but at the same time—in their desire to destroy each other —they played havoc with the emotions of their offspring. Soon, all members of the family sought counseling. They simply were unable to cope with the turmoil engendered by the divorce.

Reaction of the Children *of unfriendly divorce*

If you are a child caught up in such a whirlwind, what can you do? A teenager is not completely helpless. You have to know when to speak and when to be quiet. You need to develop almost a sixth sense about how to relate to your parents. If your mother screams accusations about your dad, it might be well to be quiet until the storm abates. Then, when your mother has calmed down somewhat, you could tell her that you love her and that you also love your father, and you hope that things can be more peaceful. You might also say that you can understand why she is so upset, since dad has not been regular in the support payments. You might even be able to say, if you catch mom in a rare good mood, that maybe she and dad ought to meet somewhere—perhaps in a restaurant—and discuss what is going on. It would be well to follow a similar procedure when you are with your father. You might point out that mom is naturally irritable since she has to take care of the children 24 hours a day whereas he only sees them on weekends. You might suggest that your father call your mother and speak directly to her, since you find it difficult to be a messenger and go-between for them. Always stress the fact that you love your dad, and that he could make things much easier for all concerned if he would try to meet your mom and thus keep in touch, so that mutual problems could be better resolved. Remember that in this modern age parents often listen to their children. Ours is a youth-oriented society in which there is respect for what a child wants and thinks. Even though a parent might reply, "But you don't know how much she hurt me . . ." you may still find that your words will in time make an impression on your parent. Deep down, most people wish to live with a minimum of pain and discord. If a parent can be shown how destructive his or her conduct is, there could be a chance to resolve at least some of the conflict and tension. It is certainly worth a try. When speaking to your parents, make clear that you understand their pain but that you also are suffering. Few parents will be unmoved by the words and tears of their children. Quarrels may be put aside when the parent finally becomes aware that his or her conduct is destroying the children. The parent that wins in the battle for the child's affection is usually the one who does the least name-calling. Initially, the parent who attacks the other seems to be the victor, but seldom is this a final victory. The decent parent who refrains from attacks has a better chance to relate positively to the child. Words are weapons and when spoken in anger can be totally destructive. But words can also heal. There are things that you as a young person can do. You do not have to be the center of the storm, nor need you be the message-bearer for parents who cannot talk to each other. You can refuse to be the one in the middle. In time, if the parents lack a messenger, they will be forced to speak to each other—unless they truly enjoy speaking only through their individual attorneys. As a young person, if your words are sensible they will eventually create a favorable climate. It may be a long time before your parents come to see that you are speaking words of wisdom, but it is certainly worth trying.

Be Wary

It is important to take what your parents say with a grain of salt. Remember that they often speak in anger as they court your sympathy and support. In an unfriendly divorce, each parent believes that he or she has been grievously wronged. Each tries to get back at the other, and the easiest way to do this is through the children. You may find you are being courted as an ally against the other parent. Do not fall into this trap. If your mother berates your father in your presence, it is best to keep quiet. If you must speak, say, "But, mom, I know you are upset, and dad is also upset. That is probably why you have difficulty communicating. You should know that it is very upsetting to us, and we do hope that you soon will find a way to talk so that problems can be solved. We love you both very much, and whatever you say—out of the pain of the moment—we will try to understand." It may not be easy to say this to your mother or father. However, if you can—in your own words —let them know that you really care and that ,you feel they are capable of getting along in a civil way without using you, then you may have a chance of success. Bitterness only begets more bitterness. If you agree with the attacker, you only encourage him or her to promote further attacks. Parents who are caught up in a bitter divorce struggle often say things they do not mean; it is anger that is speaking, not the person. Be on the alert for this and try to appreciate the fact that when one is upset one often tries deliberately to hurt another person.

You as a child must be wary and try not to be used as a weapon to destroy someone else. If your parents see how unhappy you are and that you are not sympathizing with either one of them, their conduct may change. When a person is angry, he cannot think. You can be a calming influence in a tense and bitter situation. Or if you cannot find the right words, you can just hug your mom and dad and say—with feeling—"I love both you and dad. Why can't we all find a way to be happy?" A remark such as this may help to defuse a tense moment and lead to some honest reflection and reconsideration.

If you, as a teenager, are the oldest child in the household, you can have a positive effect on your younger brothers or sisters. If they see that you are not caught up in the parental struggle and vindictiveness, they may be able to avoid being used as pawns in the parents' tug-of-war for the affection of the children.

Seeking Help

If there is an unfriendly divorce and your home situation becomes intolerable, what can you do? You have tried your best to remain level-headed and be a stabilizing force, but you find that your mother is constantly nervous and irritated. You are blamed for everything that goes wrong in the house. Nothing that you do is right. What can you do? There are some outlets for your feelings.

If you have a close friend or friends, you should certainly talk to them. A listening ear is vital. You need to unburden yourself. A good friend need not answer; just knowing that there is someone to talk to can be comforting. If you are friendly with someone who comes from a divorce situation, you can encourage that person to unburden himself or herself. Don't force it. Let the words come naturally. If you see your friend is unhappy, you can say, "I can tell by your expression that something is bothering you. Would you like to talk about it?" Just these few words may serve to get your friend to speak. It is always good to have a shoulder to lean on.

Another possible source of help could be a sympathetic adult. Perhaps there is a teacher at school, or the family doctor, or your clergyperson. Few of us can bear the burdens of life alone. Life is truly with people. Others can give support to the troubled young person who lives in a tense home. Be aware that you are only one person. You can do only so much. Unless others wish to change, or have the potential to change, you cannot effect a miraculous cure. Change is often gradual. Realization seldom comes in a dramatic flash of lightning. People tend to change when their situation becomes completely unacceptable. The human body can stand only so much punishment. Those who punish others eventually come to see that it does not bring relief. The constant "downing" of the mate solves nothing. Anger eats us up and does not generate any real accomplishments. To be human is to suffer, but to be human is also to love and to try.

It does no good to retreat into a shell. Some children do retreat into the world of fantasy and wish that all could be different. Wishing will not make it so. The reality of a bad divorce is real enough. There is no effective retreat. Perpetual silence in the face of anger is no answer. Life is with people, and we cannot escape problems.

Not only are problems to be faced, but one must also understand that life moves in cycles. One day things are truly bad, the next day they can improve. The unfriendly divorce can initially breed all sorts of personal and emotional stresses and strains. However, even as there is a limit to human endurance, so too are there limits to continuous pain. The mind and body rebel against such onslaughts. Because you are young (in years or in spirit) you will, as a normal human being, seek moments and places of pleasure. Few are completely crushed by a bitter divorce. Most of us have the inner stamina and fortitude to rise above misery. To live forever with a dejected countenance is not what most of us want. We seek a measure of happiness. Laughter and humor are often the best medicine.

A Big Brother or Big Sister

If you are a teenager and you want to do something truly worthwhile, you might investigate the social services agency in your community with a view toward becoming a big brother or a big sister to a child from a home that lacks a father or mother.

Children need both a male and female figure with whom to identify. A boy needs a father to go with him to a scout meeting or take him to a little league ballgame. A girl may lack contact with a mother to go shopping and just to engage in girl talk and share common interests. If you are a big brother to a child for a number of years, as he grows, you will grow as well. You will, in effect, learn what it is to be a good parent.

It is to be noted that there are a host of young people who need big brothers and sisters. Some of these youngsters come from divorce situations or from homes where one of the parents has passed away. In some cases, the child is being raised by a relative because the natural father and mother are separated. If you are the product of a healthy family environment, you can show the youngster that there are many happy homes that produce happy children who—in turn—will one day have happy homes of their own.

Frequently teenagers say, "I have nothing to do." Well, it is possible even for one as young as 15 to become a big brother to a child of 9 or 10. It can be a lot of fun, too. Of course to do this, your own parents have to cooperate and possibly chauffeur you and your young charge around until you are old enough to drive a car. It can be done. You will find that as you give of yourself in such a project, you will win a lifelong friend. The rewards are not monetary, but they are emotional and spiritual.

Being a big brother or sister does not mean that you will become a "mom" or a "dad" to a younger child. It means that you have the chance to make life a bit brighter for a child who could use a helping hand. You can help bring out the essential goodness in that youngster and impart some of the enthusiasm and spirit that the child needs. Most of us take it for granted that we will have someone to go swimming with, to attend a ballgame, to go to a park or to a movie. We do not realize that there are youngsters who have few such opportunities. Nothing is more rewarding than seeing the expression in the eyes of a child who knows that he is accepted and that he has in effect a second home and other people who love him. The most precious thing you can give to another person is the time you are willing to spend with that individual. That is why it is good to have friends. A true friend is someone whom you can count on. As a teenager you can make a contribution to a happier society by working with a child whose home life is not complete and who needs an older male or female role model to help him or her to develop into a worthy citizen.

Yes, You Can

The easiest thing in the world is to say, "There is nothing I can do." If your parents are divorced, you do not have to be the scapegoat and bear all the hurt and guilt. Try to realize that you did not cause the divorce. Your parents brought you into this world. Somewhere along the way they decided to separate. Not even the wisest person can fully understand why people act as they do. But if you find that you are being used as a "tool" to strike at either your father or mother, the warning buzzer should go off in your mind. Try not to be used. It will only lead to personal feelings of bitterness.

Anger seldom motivates us to achieve very much in life. In fact, it makes us lazy. Instead of trying to improve our situation, we sit around and stew in our anger. Then we can feel self-righteous. Anger immobilizes us and prevents us from acting. There is such a thing as righteous anger, which can impel us to want to make things better. I am not talking about that type of anger, but about the anger that leads nowhere. It is the anger that wells up in a bitterly contested divorce, when each party is out to get the other for wrongs either real or imagined. In such cases, there is a danger that you will be caught up in the tide of hatred and overidentify with the feelings of one of your parents. You become angry because they are angry. Yet, the anger will not solve problems and will not help you get better grades in school. To the contrary, it can even hurt your schoolwork and blunt your efforts to succeed. If a parent tries to make you his or her ally so as to "get" the other parent, be aware of what is happening. Try not to become the ally of either parent. Seek to be objective. Attempt to reason things out. If you do, you will find that it is not the people who are to blame so much as the situation itself. Adults often succumb to foolish actions because of the pressures and disappointments of life. Divorced parents are under more than the usual stresses and strains. Divorce creates problems that often seem unsolvable.

As a teenager, you may be able to be more objective than your divorcing parents. You will often see that neither of them is really at fault. Perhaps your father is angry because he cannot support two households. Your mother is depressed because she feels alone and robbed of male companionship. Grandparents feel that they are threatened with the loss of grandchildren. A host of difficulties are spawned by divorce. Sometimes the problems become too much. So try to keep in mind that when there is a painful adjustment, it is natural to blame the other party for the difficulties.

Of course, you are not superhuman, and your best efforts may appear fruitless. Yet, if you persist and remain a loving, caring person to both parents and to the grandparents, in time there is a chance that some healing and happiness can emerge. It is difficult to remain angry if the other person is loving and caring.

We are dealing with the human situation. People are not always kind, and circumstances can bring out the worst in us. Tragically, children can become victims. Resist being bitter, if you can, while being aware that as human beings we are all limited. Listen to what is said and try to distinguish what is spoken in anger from what is spoken with a degree of reasonableness and truth.

A Good Divorce?

Social critics argue as to whether or not there is such a thing as a "good" divorce. What do we mean by the term "good"? I suppose that a friendly divorce is the nearest thing to a good divorce. Every divorce causes dislocation and tends to be upsetting. When children are involved, they are a constant reminder that in some way the parents have failed. No one wishes to be reminded of failure, which is perhaps one of the reasons that the child may make the parent feel guilty about entering into divorce. Divorce does mean separation. Marriage was a coming together. Marriage involves the hopes and dreams of two persons who care about each other very deeply. Then, when living together produces disharmony and disfunction, we move into the area where separation is considered. The establishing of a new home after the first home fails is seldom easily accomplished. Divorce involves a tearing apart. It is no wonder that nerves are on edge and tension mounts. Divorce is often the last answer to a disastrous family situation. Few contemplate divorce in a lighthearted or flippant mood. Despite the fact that divorce is so common, it is not something that anyone wants or desires. A good divorce, then, can be defined as a situation in which all parties realize that it is inevitable and that life must go on with as few recriminations as possible. If basic respect remains after love is gone, new relationships can be more easily formed. Few people feel good about their divorce. They accept the reality of it and try to establish new relationships that are more satisfactory. Life does go on. We cope with divorce on the basis of what strengths we possess.

Thought Questions

1. Do you think divorce can ever be friendly? Do you have friends whose parents were divorced? Have they ever discussed how "friendly" the procedure was?
2. Why do you think so many divorces are unfriendly? Need they be so bitter?
3. What are some of the danger signals that might alert a child that a divorce is coming?
4. What can a child do to be helpful when his or her parents are about to divorce?
5. Why is it said that children are helpless in a situation where the parents are breaking up?
6. What could you do as a big brother or big sister to help a child who lives in a single-parent family?

CHAPTER VII

Should Marriages Break Up?

One of the troubling problems that confront society centers around the question of whether or not marriages should ever be dissolved. The Catholic Church has taken a firm stand on this question. For many Catholics, the dissolution of a marriage is a truly grave matter. If the marriage is not annulled according to Church law, the communicant cannot receive many of the sacraments of the Church. Although some dioceses are more liberal than others, there is still a definite procedure that must be followed before a marriage can be terminated. Catholicism takes seriously the words, "until death do us part." For the Catholic, the biblical injunction that the partners become as one—one in body, in spirit, and in flesh—is not taken lightly.

The world is changing, however, and the unchallengeable view of marriage as the firm bulwark of society is no longer fully accepted by all segments of society. Spokespersons have stepped forward to proclaim that there are specific situations in which the marriage should end.

First, let us consider the arguments of those who look upon marriage as indissoluble. What do they have to say?

A Commitment Must Be Taken Seriously

Proponents of "stay together at any cost" hold that we live in times when too many promises are broken. Marriage is a serious matter. It should be entered into after much thought. The couple should not only be in love but should have resolved all doubts as to the seriousness of their commitment. In sickness and in health, the vows are fashioned. Until death do us part becomes the spoken or unspoken command. As one flesh, the couple is to realize that this is not a light or trivial matter. Once the vows are exchanged, the partners are to remain in the marriage for better or for worse. If difficulties arise, they must be solved within the marriage and not in the office of an attorney. A sobbing woman in my office once said, "Dr. Raab, I just cannot understand Henry. When we married I decided that no matter what happened, I would never leave him. I never considered divorce, despite the difficulties of our marriage. Now my husband has gone to a lawyer. I cannot understand his thinking. When we got married he promised it would be forever. We have three children. What am I going to do? I have built my life around my husband and children. He says he cannot continue to live with us. The other day he got very angry, packed his bags, and walked out. I am really desperate. I cannot understand him. Isn't marriage to be forever? You don't just walk away from responsibility. I think he must be sick. I told him to see a psychiatrist, but he just laughed and said, 'There's nothing wrong with me.' "

Couples who hold to what has been termed the traditional view of marriage will, in truth, wish to "stick it out," even if it is a bad marriage.

For the Sake of the Children

Bill and Jean are seated in my office. They look very sad. Bill speaks: "Dr. Raab, the spark has gone out of our relationship. We have two wonderful kids. Jean and I love them very much. We feel we are good parents. But our attitudes toward each other are not healthy. The love we shared just is not there. We seldom make love. Whatever pleasure is left in the marriage comes from the achievements of the kids. Our children are rapidly approaching the time when they will become teenagers. We do not wish to destroy our home. We have had counseling, and so far nothing seems to help. Our marriage has turned sour. It is just blah. We wonder what will happen if we stick it out, and then when the kids are grown up and gone what will we have? We will be left staring at each other over the breakfast dishes, with nothing to talk about. Maybe we should make the break now, while we still have some youthful years left. We were very young when we got married. We would not listen to our parents, who told us to wait so as to be sure. We were the first in our crowd to go down the aisle. Now we feel that we have missed something. I am not sure what it is." Jean was sitting and sobbing softly while her husband spoke. She seemed confused and dazed by it all. Perhaps with counseling and time, the spark of love could be rekindled. It would be a difficult process but worth attempting.

Bill and Jean have a devitalized relationship. The living "juices" of excitement and discovery have been blunted by the sameness and routine of everyday life. The one bright light in their lives is parenthood. They are also concerned about their in-laws. Bill and Jean feel that they have an obligation to their children and to the grandparents. They see themselves as part of a social structure, so they are willing to set aside personal feelings for the sake of their offspring. Bill says, "How do I know I will be any happier if I leave Jean and try to make a new life for myself? I hate the thought of being alone and not seeing my children every day. Even though Jean and I have a brother-sister type of marriage, maybe that is all most people have. I guess I am an incurable romantic. When deep physical love faded away, I became restless. I kept asking, 'What else is there in life?' I am not sure our friends are any happier than we are. They, too, are playing the marriage game as they put on a good act. I wonder what really goes on behind closed doors in their homes. Just from the little I hear and expressions I see, I have a strong feeling that no one is really that happy. At the moment, we just seem to be drifting along without any real goals. It's as if we are waiting for something wonderful to happen—as if we hope for the magic fairy to wave a wand over us and restore our lost love for each other. There are no magic potions. Life is dull and predictable. I wonder how long this can go on?"

Jean finally speaks up, as she brushes the tears from her eyes: "I don't know what to do. I try to keep a neat home. Dinner is always on the table when he comes home. I have taught the children to respect their father. I try to keep myself attractive. I don't know what Bill expects of me. Maybe I am not passionate enough or warm enough for him. My mother often told me that I was a cold fish. Maybe she was right. I cannot fake my feelings. I do love Bill, but I am a bit shy in expressing myself. We have had counseling, and we have tried to make our marriage better. So far, things are pretty much the same. Bill is right. Much of our marriage is blah. Yet we do love our kids, and for their sake I doubt if we will split up. I could not face the children and tell them that we are breaking up. My kids are sensitive and trusting. It would destroy them. I have seen too many mixed-up kids from broken homes.

"Our children are doing well in school, and they have lovely friends. We live in a pleasant neighborhood. I guess we should count our blessings and not expect more than that. When you bring children into the world, you have an obligation to take care of them. How can one parent raise children without a father? It can't be good. I will not put the kids through such a wringer unless Bill insists. If he really decides he wants a divorce, there is not much else I can do. But I would hate to face my own parents and tell them I have failed in marriage. Divorce is failure, you know."

Jean's voice trailed off and was inaudible. Bill sat uncomfortably in the chair, staring off into space. It was as if he were not in the room. The couple had stopped communicating. If they could be brought to the point where they would talk directly to each other, perhaps some progress could be made. In their case, divorce had been ruled out as an option. At least that is what they said, albeit with some hesitation. They wanted to make their marriage work. Because of the children, they would not seriously consider going to an attorney to begin divorce proceedings.

There are many Bill-Jean couples in society who do keep their marriages intact and hope for the best. They never give up hope that things will somehow change and that time will solve most problems. Sometimes such couples say, "Sex is not that important. It is overrated. We don't have sex that often, and when we do it really isn't much fun. But, so what? There is more to life than going to bed with someone. We have the kids, our home, and our friends. Things will work out. Besides, who is perfect? Who is to say that if we split and remarry we will find more fulfillment the second time around?" Such couples can point to statistics showing that second marriages do not usually fare much better than first marriages.

Love Is Overrated

Bill and Jean, like many couples, have concluded that love is not the most vital ingredient in marriage. This view manifests itself in any number of ways. Sometimes a wife (or husband) will hold on to a marriage even when the partner is unfaithful. One wife said, "I know that my husband is more passionate than I am. He has a tremendous appetite for sex. Frankly, he wears me out. I know that no woman can really satisfy him. So, when he goes on a business trip, I doubt that he remains faithful. I really do not want to know about his escapades. I prefer not to hear about them. Well-meaning friends have dropped hints about his extracurricular love-making. I shut my ears, and I would never confront him with accusations. Suppose I hired a detective and got the goods on him; then what? I could demand a divorce and a big settlement, but would that make me happy? Deep down, I still love the guy, with all his faults. He is a good father and an excellent provider. No one is perfect. Sex is his weakness. No woman could satisfy him very long. As long as he comes back to me, I will be here. In time, as we grow old together, his sex drive will slacken, and I will have him, the kids, the home, and our friends. Sure, many of my so-called friends think I am a fool. I must admit that sometimes it hurts to know how he acts. But, there are men who are a lot worse. Besides, men have greater sex appetites than we do. My mother taught me this. She was a wise old lady. What is true love? I am not sure anybody really knows what it is.

Young people live together to try each other out. Is that love? Will they have better marriages if they try sex before the wedding? From what my friends tell me, their kids have lived with future spouses, but then—after they stand at the altar—the marriage still breaks up. Our society has glorified sex and made it too important. I will not be trapped by those who say that love is everything. I love my husband, and I feel that in his own way he loves me too. Maybe love is the wrong word—he likes me. We are good friends. What is the big deal about sex? When we were first married, we hardly got out of bed the first year. Then things cooled off. I imagine the same thing happens to most people. Anyway, it's a man's world. You can't tell me that the average businessman who is on the road is faithful to the little lady back home. If she is wise, she will not ask too many questions." The wife in this case has downgraded the importance of physical love. She sees no reason to break up her marriage because of this one major "flaw" in her husband's personality.

For her—and many others—the fear of loneliness and rejection is worse than having an unfaithful mate. I once counseled a troubled husband who had discovered that his wife was unfaithful. He said, "I guess I am different from most guys. I have never strayed, even though there have been lots of chances. In my office in the city, the girls don't even ask a guy if he is married. They just go after any available pair of pants. Me, I must be different. I really love my wife and kids. Then I found out that my wife has been playing around with one of the guys in her office, a married man with children. When I confronted her with it, she said, "Yes, it's true. I don't love him, but I do find him nice.' She says she still loves me, but she wants some variety in her life. At first I was very angry with her and with him. I thought of suing for divorce, but now I find I want her even more than before. It's strange, Dr. Raab. I should hate her and this other guy, but I find I love her a whole lot. It is as if two guys are dating the same girl and vying for her affection. Is there something wrong with me? What should I do?" The love pattern described in this instance is truly perplexing. After counseling many troubled couples, one discovers that physical love is not always the central factor that leads to divorce. My guess is that many couples have downgraded it, despite the media campaign that says "love is everything." Couples are able to attain varying degrees of happiness and togetherness even in situations in which one mate is unfaithful and the other knows of it.

Another common situation is as follows. An attractive middle-aged woman comes into the office. She talks at length about the problems in her marriage. Finally, she looks directly at me and says, "You

know, Dr. Raab, love is not everything. At my age, what would I do
if I got a divorce? I am not the Club-Med type, flying off to Europe
or an island for a fast romance. Besides, I'm too old for all that. I
have seen my divorced friends. After the split, they slim down, get
new clothes, have a face-lift and a new hairdo, and then they start
chasing after men. When they see they cannot land a guy their own
age, they go after older or younger guys. All they talk about is men.
It is sickening. They are so unhappy behind the masks they wear. I
could never shack up with a man in order to land him. When you are
single, all the men want is one thing, and most girls are willing to
give it to them. I am not the type for one-night stands. I shall hold on
to him even though he strays quite a bit. I need the guy, even though
he breaks my heart."

Keeping Up Appearances

Some marriages are other-directed. By this I mean that some
people live only to please society. They are fearful that if they break
the mores or codes of the social system, something terrible will occur.
It is not so much a matter of keeping up with the neighbors as to
maintain a facade that "all is well." For example, a couple sits before me. The wife begins: "Dr. Raab, we are not youngsters. I was
taught as a girl that certain things were proper and other things
should be avoided. My parents prided themselves on the fact that
there had never been a divorce in our family for three generations. It
was pounded into my head that when I married I would make my
bed and sleep in it—forever. If I made the wrong choice, there was
to be no escape. I could not disgrace the family. I know this seems
silly today, and the notion is certainly not modern. What is worse, I
really have no restraints on my conduct, since my parents died years
ago. Still, what they taught me continues to guide my life. John and
I have always tried to keep up appearances. No matter how rocky
the road of marriage proved to be, we resolved that we would stick
it out. As far as our friends are concerned, we are the happiest and
best-adjusted couple in our crowd. We are always together at every
social function. We never take separate vacations, and there has
never been a hint of scandal. Many times our friends have confided
in us that their marriages were shaky and asked us for the secret of
our success. We could never tell them that we are merely actors.
What others think is really very important to us. Even though we are
miserable much of the time, we would never seriously contemplate a
divorce. It does get difficult at times, but we manage to hide our
emotions. At times I would like to just scream to hell with it, but that

would not be proper. No one would understand. After all, we are a model couple and our kids are model children."

The husbands responds, "Mary is right. We began life with a very proper wedding with our very proper friends. We planned an orderly life together and established modest goals. Everything should have worked out fine, since everyone said we were ideally suited for each other. That was part of the problem. Everyone had told us for so long that we were perfect for each other that in time we came to believe it. Instead of thinking for ourselves, we sort of fell into a pattern. All our friends were pairing off. We were the last two left unmarried in our group, so we sort of drifted into marriage. Our whole life has been a struggle to keep up appearances. We have striven to live in the best part of town, have the classiest cars, and send our kids to the best camps and schools. I know it sounds trite to speak of such behavior, and it may seem a little odd to admit it, but we tend to be more surface than substance. Well, our marriage is foundering on the rocks of bitter arguments and much quarreling. I find that the pressure to keep up with the country-club crowd is just too much. I have become more than a social drinker, and I have lots of problems at the office. Younger men are crowding me, and I just don't know how much longer I will be able to hold on to my job. I know that my wife tries to be sympathetic, but it looks now as if our whole world is crumbling. What can we do?"

At one time it was usual for people who were upwardly mobile to concentrate more on what others thought than on their own standards, desires, and wishes. Even today, appearance does count. If you, as a teenager, are applying for a job, you know that messy long hair and blue jeans are not likely to win you an appointment. People are judged as much by how they look as by what they know. You can be the smartest person in the world, but if you don't look the part, your chances of finding employment in most fields will be very slim. So, in a society that places so much emphasis on appearance, it is not surprising that some families are built around the image of what the community thinks is best. In a sense, this may not be bad. For example, if you are naturally sloppy and you move into an area where everyone keeps a neatly trimmed lawn, community pressure can monitor and change your conduct. It is necessary to maintain standards of decent conduct, and we do need role models to emulate. The danger may come when we decide that whatever the community decides is right and that we must follow the whim, fashion, and style of the crowd. Some families have evolved a certain image, and they will follow it right or wrong. If the style of the group demands acting a certain way, they will conform. I recall a woman who said, "We moved to Florida and were surprised to find that the best people took their kids to McDonald's for hamburgers on week nights. Naturally, we have done the same thing with our youngsters." This woman was very fad-conscious. She had to be sure she was behaving, acting, and dressing in a way that indicated she knew the social demands of the community.

If you act a role, that role may in time become the real you. Or you may never know who is the real you. On a television talk show, a famous star was being interviewed. He was asked, "Tell us, who is the real you? Are you an author, a director, or an actor?" The man thought for a moment and then replied, "It's funny that you should ask me such a question. I am not really sure who I am. I guess I am whatever part I happen to be playing at a given moment."

It Could Be Worse

Some people have a genuine fear of divorce. In their view, it would be really terrible if their marriage were to end in divorce. A young wife says, "I have seen many of my friends who really did not give their marriage a chance. At the first hint of trouble, the girl ran home to daddy and the boy ran home to mamma. Many of my friends are really quite immature. I often wonder why they bothered to get married in the first place. I guess being married is still the "in" thing. Our generation likes to try everything, be it liquor, drugs, or marriage. Then, when kids do get married, they feel trapped. Herb and I are different. We have been married for six years. We have had lots of problems. Actually, there are very few things we enjoy doing together. We still have good sex, but not much else. I refuse to allow myself to get pregnant, because I am not really sure that our marriage will make it. I do not want to be burdened with a child. It costs money to raise a child, and if things don't work out I would have plenty of trouble landing another guy with a kid hanging around my neck. I am not about to have a kid so that my mother can become a grandmother. If I want to have a kid, it will be because I want the kid, not because my folks or my in-laws feel it is about time that we started a family. Yes, we have lots of problems. But my philosophy is that it could be worse. I can remember how lonely I was as a child. My parents were cold fish. I married Herb because he came from a warm and loving family. But apparently I can't give Herb the loving affection he craves. He has accused me of being cold and unfeeling. We are going for counseling, and we may end up at a sex-adjustment clinic. At times I feel we are going through a living hell. But, as bad as it is, I know it could be much worse. If we split, what would happen to me? I could never go back to my parents. We do not communicate. My dad sits in front of the TV day and night; he scarcely talks. My mother is a social butterfly. She always was working for wonderful causes but never had time for her own kids. We were like little orphans. Mom was out to save the world, but she lost her own children. So I was glad when Herb proposed marriage. I really wanted to escape from my home, but that was not a good reason to get married. Still, I plan to stick it out. I have known much worse times than now. Maybe counseling will help me become a warmer, more loving wife. If that occurs, then Herb and I could be really happy."

The belief that it "could be worse" is heard in many quarters. Couples see marriages crumbling all around them. They see their friends, now divorced, drifting into the uncertainties of the singles scene. The divorced seem to be scarred, scared, and unhappy. We live in a coupled society. It is better to seek the safe harbor and sanctuary of marriage than to be adrift on a sea of aloneness. Why take a chance? Even in a bad marriage, we know what we have. At least there is another warm body in the house. And who knows, perhaps things will get better.

A couple come into my office. They are newlyweds but are very unhappy. He works on the night shift, and she works days. They literally pass each other coming and going. Their children are confused, since they only see their parents together on weekends. The husband has always been a night person. He lacks ambition and would not want to work days. The couple lived together for several months before they married. They both had young children from previous marriages. The husband complained, "My wife is moody and withdrawn. I want to be with her. After all we are newlyweds. But we are both under a lot of pressure. Her kids and my kids don't really get along. We have lots of bills to pay. I'm still paying alimony to my ex-wife, and my wife's ex-husband keeps calling her and telling her that I am not good enough for her. He is trying to ruin our marriage. It was better before we got married. We would have been better off to have a common-law relationship. The way things are now, our marriage will never make it."

The wife replies, "Irv just will not give me space. I need some moments of privacy. He is crowding me. He acts like a newlywed couple I saw on TV, where the husband was all over the wife to the extent that she could not take it. We have lots of problems. Both of us work, and we have a big mortgage on the house, plus his alimony payments. His kids and my kids have to get used to us and to each other. On top of that, with me working days and him working nights, we scarcely see each other. Our marriage is developing into a night-mare. Yet, I really do love Irv, and I know that he loves me. Despite everything, it could be worse. My first marriage was a flop, and it was largely my fault. I am bound and determined to make this marriage work. As they say, for better or for worse. At the moment, there is more 'worse' than 'better'."

Irv interjects, "Yes, Karen and I both have been burned. We came into this marriage with our eyes open. There are some really rough spots, when the noise level in the house is just too much. I console myself with the memory of my first marriage. It was an awful failure. I think I have learned from my mistakes. The trouble is, you never stop learning and you never stop making mistakes. Neither Karen nor I will even consider divorce . . . at least not now. We both know that no matter how bad it is, we still have each other, and no matter how long it takes, or how bitter the road, we will somehow make it. We know, better than most, that it was a lot worse in our previous marriages—and it would be a disaster were we to split and go our separate ways."

As you talk to couples you discover that many do take refuge in the idea that things could be worse if they were to dissolve their re-lationship. The "it could be worse" syndrome is often the glue that holds a shaky relationship together. It is certainly not the best reason to maintain a marriage, but it can provide some basis for going on when the going seems almost beyond endurance.

A Time to Part

A view that is gaining wide acceptance (if one is to judge by the rising divorce figures) is the notion that it is better to divorce than to be totally miserable. After counseling, pleading, second honey-moons, long discussions, and earnest efforts, a couple see that their relationship is empty of meaning and satisfaction, and divorce be-comes a viable option. Some marriage counselors (themselves di-vorced) may gently push the couple toward a separation. A friend confided in me in a tone of complete disgust, "Bob, you would not believe what I am about to say. I have a business associate who was dying to get out of his marriage. He was seeing this young chick, and his wife had found out about it. The wife wanted to sustain the marriage. Well, I sent the couple to a clergyperson, and he counseled them to undertake a trial separation. Now they are divorcing. The clergyperson himself was having marital troubles with his wife, and I feel that he was acting out his own problem and dumping on my associate. I was never so angry at anyone in my life. What kind of clergyperson would do such a thing?" I replied that he should not take it out on the clergy. It is quite possible that the counselor was trying to be objective, but that his own feelings and emotions got in the way. In any event, the question of when or when not to divorce can be a delicate and difficult decision. There are counselors whose basic premise is that wherever possible the couple should try to work things out rather than divorce. There are others who quickly suggest that a trial separation is in order. Since you are playing with human lives and emotions, it takes a skilled counselor to guide the couple toward the decision that is right for them.

What are the ideas of those who feel that there are situations in which marriages should break up?

Nothing in Common

A phrase often heard is encapsulated in the following comments of a distraught young wife. "Sid and I really have very little that we share. I love the opera, ballet, and concerts. He sleeps peacefully through them. Yet he is kind enough to go with me to these cultural events, even though I know he is bored stiff. His idea of an exciting Sunday afternoon is to watch the Wide World of Sports on TV. He is always watching sports events. We even subscribe to cable TV so that he can watch some sports event every day of the year. At times I would like to pull the TV plug out of the wall. It has reached the point where we have very little to say to each other. When the kids were growing up, we had a common concern in raising them. Now they are out of the house. We could be like newlyweds again if we only had more common interests."

A husband laments: "Cynthia was a lovely young girl when we were married. Now she has turned into a witch. I was raised in a house where everything was neat and in place. She was raised in a very casual home. I expect the dishes to be done as soon as we finish eating. She can leave them stacked up while she talks on the phone to her many friends. She is not in a hurry to do anything. The only time the house is straightened out is when company comes. She knows I would be happy in a neatly kept house, but that is not her style. She is a smart girl and has lots of friends. I try to be tolerant of her sloppiness, but it is getting to me. She is not careful about her personal appearance. Her trim figure is gone. She doesn't care how she looks. I hate to admit it, but she has turned into a slob. We have talked about this on many occasions. She told me that I would have to accept her as she is—that she is too old to change her ways. We have fine children, and I hate to think of divorce, but—if things don't become different, I can't see our marriage continuing."

Sociologists have pointed out that marriages often fall apart if the couple have little communication. This can occur when their interests diverge. It does not mean that they are bad or nasty. Rather, it implies that they are not concerned with the same values and pursuits. Sometimes in marriage a couple wed with the idea of changing the other person. When this fails, much misery ensues. A wife cries, "Sam is impossible. I am always picking up after him. He never remembers where he puts things. He is a rotten businessman. Half of his accounts owe him money, but he keeps such poor records that he seldom collects what is owed to him. He is always on the verge of fiscal disaster. I, on the other hand, tend to be well organized and efficient. Sam feels that what is not done today can be done tomorrow. We are not the same kind of person. I should have realized this before we got married. Now we are married and have a child. I don't feel that we should remain together. Painful as divorce might be, it is still better than what I have now. I have lost respect for Sam. When I married him I honestly thought that with love and affection I could change him. It didn't work out that way. His life-style is too deeply ingrained. Sam admits that he is hopeless. He has said that I have to accept him with his strengths and weaknesses. All I see in him is weakness. I have married a child. I wanted someone to lean on. Instead, I find that he is leaning on me. This is no way to run a marriage. I want out—as soon as possible."

When couples discover that they have little they can share, love is apt to fly out the window. Again, it must be stressed that in many divorce situations neither person is a bad guy or a good guy. People are individuals, and not every couple can work out a harmonious relationship. If all you have in common are the house and the children, it may not be enough to sustain a marital relationship. People do not think alike. Unless you are on the same or a similar wavelength your marriage could be approaching troubled waters. The bottom line of a relationship is reached when one spouse says with a sigh, "We have tried everything, but we just do not have anything in common."

Facing Adultery

The jet age has made adultery readily available. Businessmen are off on long trips overseas. Major cities offer enticing sex attractions. In Las Vegas an ad in a local magazine said, "Escorts for hire. Health certificates provided." It was obvious the type of escorts the company would provide. Much of the casino humor concerns "hookers." Sex for pay becomes an open commodity. A social researcher has categorized how attitudes have changed. In a more traditional

society, if a man had an "affair" he was very discreet about it. Today, some males (and females) flaunt their adulterous ties. They may
say, "I might as well be up front about this. Why should I keep my
actions a secret?" In earlier times a community would be scandalized.
Today, people tend to shrug their shoulders and say, "So what?"
Open solicitation is common. Couples seldom ask if the other is married. Sex for fun and emotional release is abundant. The Bible looked
upon adultery as a cardinal sin. Modern society tends to be forgiv-
ing. Even today, adultery by the male seems to be more tolerated
than adultery by the female. Males are thought by many to be more
passionate and to have greater sexual appetites. The woman is expected to be more sheltered and passive.

With all the modern attitudes, poses, and conversation, many
spouses cannot condone adultery. It strikes at the heart of a relationship. A tearful wife cries, "How could he do this to me? I always
trusted him because I know how much we love each other. He has
always been a good husband and father. We have always been affectionate to each other. I have been living in a fool's paradise. How
was I to know that he had a girl on the side? He has begged me for
forgiveness and promised it will never happen again. But if he can
be unfaithful once, how can I ever trust him in the future? Whenever
we go to bed I will have it in my mind that he is not thinking of me,
but of her. Am I foolish to be this way? Am I old-fashioned? I have
already been to see a lawyer and have been assured that I can get
substantial alimony if I wish to break up our marriage. I am at a loss
what to do. I think I still love him, but his betrayal is unforgivable. I
just can't stand to have him touch me now, after he has been with
her. I don't know how many girls he has had during our marriage."
Adultery is not easily forgiven despite the standards of the new
morality. Spouses can forgive almost everything. Sexual infidelity
may be the hardest thing to set aside. It says to a person, "I have
failed to be attractive and interesting enough to you, so you have
sought the company of others." Love is still thought by many to be
expressed most fully in the act of sex. Betrayal in this most intimate
of areas can hasten the process of divorce.

No Excitement

A husband complains, "My wife is just not interesting; she doesn't
turn me on. She is a great cook, but she is not much fun. We have
nothing to talk about, really. At night I would like to go out dancing,
but she is always too tired. At parties she always gives me the signal
that it is time to go. We are invariably the first to leave. She needs

a lot of sleep, since she is a working gal. We don't have much of a marriage. We just sort of live together. All we share are the memories of when our kids were young. Now they are grown up and have married and moved away. We have each other, and the house is really empty. I wish we could put some sparkle and excitement into our life. But I long for the early years of our marriage when we were making our plans and dreaming our dreams. Now we are into our middle years, and not much is going on. Everything is predictable. I hate to say it, but I am really bored by it all. Whether I am home or at the office it makes little difference. I dread going home to such a dreary, uninspired life. I guess I am just as much to blame as she is. Our friends tell us how lucky we are. They should only know."

Today's world stresses the new and the innovative. In a changing world, we tend to tire of things easily. The latest fad, food, or mode of dress is quickly replaced by something else. We burn out our interest in things and in people at a rapid rate. It becomes very difficult to keep up with the many developments that spring into the headlines. One day we read of the possibility of the cloning of a man. Another day a headline proclaims the birth of the first test-tube baby. The novel is news. A man is sued by his cousin because he refuses to donate bone marrow for a transplant; the court decides that a human being cannot be forced to donate a part of his body, even though it is desperately needed to save the life of another. As is so often the case, science is ahead of the moral and ethical demands of our culture. Is there an ethical dimension to the problem of the test-tube baby? Some religious and civil authorities think so. We are in the age of the most rapid of changes, and it is hard to know what to do and what to believe.

It is no wonder that we seek new thrills, new people, and new places to visit and to live. Ours is a constantly mobile society that is impatient with the status quo. Marriage means commitment and a feeling that there is permanence to relationships. Thus it flies in the very face of the world that swirls around us. Unhappy? Fly away (if you can afford it) to some new island for adventure and fun. Escape is always possible from every situation. Some flee from responsibility. A husband declares, "I have had it. I am fed up with the bills, the responsibilities, my job, the kids, and my wife and in-laws. I just want to be alone for a while. Too much is happening, and it is occurring too darn fast. I feel I am being pressured to death. I just cannot escape. Besides, I feel I am getting stale at my work. I do the same dull things day after day. How I long for something fresh, exciting, and really new. I need something or someone to believe in. The world is so full of phoniness." The same lament is echoed by the wife, who says, "Housework is dull, dull, dull. The kids scream all day. I am trapped in this house. How I wish we had waited longer before having kids. My husband is out with interesting people. I am stuck in this place. I am sick of listening to the talk and whining of my three-year-old. How dull it is to be at home with a kid!" Being trapped in a boring routine in the office or the home can be very debilitating. It is no wonder that some look to divorce as a way to escape from the humdrum routine of daily living.

Our world is predicated on the assumption that life should be zesty, exhilarating, and ever new. The dull is to be endured. The novel and different are to be sought. We like exciting people to do stimulating things with us. Marriage may seem placid and dull to those who need constant stimulation. Living in an age of hyperactivity puts still further strain upon the modern marriage.

The Reality Factor

We see that in our society divorce is very much on the increase. Few families are untouched by this phenomenon. It is obvious that a majority of Americans look upon divorce as a viable option when a marriage begins to encounter stormy weather. Our age puts great stress on personal happiness and fulfillment. When our partners do not make us happy, we begin to look elsewhere for that elusive someone who can bring us what we most desire. People today are given to the concept of variety. We easily tire of our jobs, our possessions, and—for many—even of our mates. The question whether marriages should break up is being answered every day by the vast numbers who are in touch with their lawyers, and it is reflected in the crowded court calendars. Divorce has become almost as much a way of life as is marriage. Despite religious objections and cultural and social pressures, the urge to break up is insatiable. For some, divorce is unthinkable for social, economic, or ethical and moral reasons. Some hold that marriages must be sustained, because the alternative is bound to be much worse. Most, however, are of the opinion that bad marriages are worse for the parents and the children. An increasingly large number are willing to take their chances with the often painful process of divorce.

Despite the bitterness and guilt that can be engendered, today's American by and large has not ruled out divorce as an alternate lifestyle. Most social thinkers concur that if a marriage is really destructive to the parties involved, it should be terminated. Critics of such a view hold that a bad marriage is better than a good divorce. Studies of children who are the products of divorced parents are inconclusive.

What does seem apparent is that the children are forced to grow up more quickly, and their maturity level rises as they see what is occurring to them and to their parents. No one really welcomes divorce, but the social stigma has lessened. A woman remarks, "When I told my friends that my daughter was getting a divorce, there was almost no reaction. It was as if they were saying, 'So what else is new?' " The sheer numbers involved make divorce more acceptable to society. Few would say it is desirable, but it is rapidly becoming a sociological and cultural fact of life in 20th-century living. From my own experience in working with many troubled couples, I have come to the sad conclusion that if all else has failed and the couple cannot resolve differences, divorce becomes the answer. I would stress that all other options should be exhausted; e.g., counseling, second honeymoon, long serious talks with family and friends, and any other approaches that might save the relationship. I would caution couples not to seek legal advice until all avenues of reconciliation have been explored. The young adult in the family might be able to be supportive if the parents ask, "What do you think about our going for marriage counseling?" If you can be supportive in efforts to save the marriage, then by all means do so!

Thought Questions

1. Should a marriage be held together despite internal problems?
2. How can one tell if a marriage should or should not be terminated?
3. Why are marriages maintained for the sake of the children? Is that a good thing to do?
4. Why are people so afraid to live alone after a divorce?
5. How important is it for a marriage to be exciting and full of fun?
6. What is meant when a couple say they have nothing in common with each other? Why does this lead to divorce?

CHAPTER VIII

Alternatives to Divorce

It might be well to consider some of the suggestions to stem the rising tide of divorce. We live in an age of alternatives. The phrase "alternate life-styles" has gained wide-ranging acceptance. What are some of the ways in which divorce can be avoided? *

Living Together

There are young couples who have decided that marriage is a barrier to happiness. A young woman declares, "Joe and I have lived together for four years. I am not really sure that we will ever get married. Our relationship does not have to be formalized by a piece of paper. Love is not a matter of legal constraints. Each of us is free to leave whenever we desire to do so. But it's a funny thing, in our case the very absence of pressure to stay together seems to make it easier for us to be together. We have many married friends, and they are not doing as well as we are. In fact, several of them have divorced. We are very happy the way things are. If we decide to have kids, then we will think about marriage. Living together is the accepted life-style today. Yes, it is awkward sometimes, when we are out socially in a strange crowd and people discover we are not married; but this is only a problem when we are with older people. With people our own age, many are living the same way we are. Joe and I feel very fulfilled. Sure, we have our quarrels, but we quickly make up. At least for now, neither one of us is pushing for marriage. We have seen too many marriages bust up. Joe and I have lots in common. Love—and not marriage—is the bond that keeps us together."

Joe speaks up: "My parents are not comfortable with the arrangement that Jane and I have. They belong to a different generation. And I know Jane's parents would be a lot happier if we were married. They worry about their little girl getting pregnant. My folks are

---

* Much of the material in this chapter was based on ideas found in Karl Fleischmann's fine article titled "Marriage by Contract: Defining the Terms of Relationship." (Reprint from the *Family Law Quarterly*, Volume 8, Number 1, Spring 1974.

more concerned about trying to explain their son's life-style to their friends. They try to act cool about it all, but I can tell that they are not too happy about the way we live. It is harder on the older generation. For them, love and sex must be within the framework of marriage. Jane and I do not subscribe to this notion. My dad said he could never have lived with mom before marriage. It simply was not done in those days. Well, times have changed. Just about everyone we know lived together before marriage—if, indeed, they decided to wed at all."

Living together is not condemned by society. Almost daily one opens a newspaper to read of a celebrity who travels with someone, and there is no commitment to marriage. A young man declares, "I want to make sure that Helen is right for me, and I am right for her. I am not exploiting her, and she is not exploiting me. If we fall out of love, then we simply part. Why get married? Many in my generation believe that marriage ruins a love relationship. Suddenly the responsibilities and the pressures rise. Who needs such a thing? We are happy and are enjoying unwedded bliss. There are no in-law hassles to contend with, since we have not marched down the aisle. Also, we do not have to be concerned with our folks giving us a big expensive wedding. We will leave things the way they are."

Living together can be a prelude to marriage. For others, it is just a state of adjustment in which to find love and companionship. It may even be looked upon as a trial marriage, without the permanency that the marriage vows imply.

Not to Marry at All

Another variation on this life-style is to retain independent living quarters and not to enter into living-together arrangements. A young man declares: "Marriage is just not for me. Maybe I am a prude, but I do not want to have a girl move in with me. I prefer my freedom. There is lots to do and to see in the world. As a bachelor, I can pack my bags anytime and change jobs or go on a trip. My financial obligations are minimal, and I can be a free soul. At my age, it is easy to find temporary companions—for a night or for a week. I like to be on the go, and I am not ready to settle down. I may never be in the mood to make a commitment to one person. So far, I have avoided long-term live-in arrangements, since they can lead to the pressure of should we or should we not get married? I really am not sure that I am the type to be a husband and father. I kind of like kids, but to bring up a child is a big expense. I have seen what kids have done to my friends' marriages. There are enough who feel as I do, so that

I am not alone. Heck, there are all sorts of singles apartments, bars, and travel groups. Singles seem to be more relaxed and less uptight. I am constantly meeting new people and having new experiences. If I ever settle down with one woman, it will be because she meets all of my expectations. For the moment, anyway, I cannot see any advantage to permanency. My parents have started to bug me about my free and easy life. They feel that a man of thirty should have a wife and kids. Somehow, they do not understand what is going on today. Things are different. It is not the same world."

As more and more opt for the single, unattached life, the sheer number of those who choose this life-style will make it easier to maintain. In addition, the ranks of "singles" are being swelled daily by the newly divorced who seek a different life-style.

Contractual Marriage

Some couples have toyed with the idea of a limited marriage contract. Under such a plan, the couple sign a mutual pact to live together for a stated number of years and during that time to avoid having children. The childless phase of the contract is subject to periodic review and can be extended or canceled depending on the wishes of the couple. After a number of childless years, the couple may decide to enter into an indefinite or permanent contract, during which time they will seek to start a family. The idea behind the contract sequence is to provide opportunities to dissolve the relationship, while at the same time to give some structure to the agreement. Proponents of this system believe that just living together is too nebulous and does not offer sufficient grounds for building a common life in a common residence. Although not recognized as a legal matter, the contract does offer some people still another alternative. Arthur speaks of this: "I know that the serial marriage contract may seem strange to some, but Sue and I are just not ready to see a clergyperson. After living together for a while, we decided to draw up a contract outlining what we expected of each other. We plan to hold to that contract for one year. If, during that time, we find it has to be revised or dropped, we will do so. We came to the conclusion that we should set something down on paper. Having something in writing gives us a basis of discussion. We can get a better idea of where we are and where we are going. Many of our friends just drift into a relationship. By committing our ideas and expectations to writing, we have a better chance of finding out what is really on our minds. This type of honesty is important if any relationship is to survive. We are trying to avoid leaving a lot of things unsaid. We know our contract cannot cover everything, but unless some duties and responsibilities are identified, nothing much can happen. The contract will give us a better idea as to whether we are suited to each other for a long-term relationship. Our parents laugh and say we are immature. They tell us that you cannot plan out everything, and that contracts for marriage are silly. We don't think so. At college we learned that we live in a contractual society. Everything we do is based on some sort of agreement, either written or verbal. No business could exist without the use of contracts. We do not feel marriage is a business, but we feel we can borrow from the world of commerce the idea of setting down what each of us can expect from the other. If it works, fine. If it doesn't work, we can either continue living together or split up. We know that a mere piece of paper will not decide the fate of our relationship, but we think it can be helpful. If it can be useful, why not give it a try?"

Some of the matters that can be considered in a contractual marriage might be the following:

Attitude Toward Personal Development. Can there be agreement on the matter of education? How does the husband feel about his wife's continuing her college training after children arrive? Will he be willing to help out in the evening while his wife is in school? A wife says, "I know that my husband is not thrilled with my going to school at night. It means he has to warm up dinner when he gets home from work. And he misses the fact that we are not together for three evenings a week. But he also realized that I was going stale being strictly a housewife. Our children are all in school now, and I want to get out more. I think that deep down he is proud of me. I know that my kids are pleased that mom is also going to school. I have a need to develop my mind. These evenings at college are the highlight of my week." It is important for husbands and wives to realize the needs of each other. Our age is very education-oriented. The housewife may long to be back in a classroom, and the colleges are responding to this need. So a contractual marriage might well define the feelings of the couple on this issue.

Socializing. How do the husband and wife feel about having friends of the same sex as well as friends of a different sex? Will the husband be jealous if his wife goes to the ballet or a concert with a man? How does the wife feel about her husband's attending luncheon conferences with his secretary? If the wife dislikes sports, would she be unhappy if her husband went to a baseball game with a female friend? It should be possible to discuss such matters. Do you have to do everything together? What are the parameters of conduct with adults outside of your home? Would your marriage be destroyed if your husband occasionally had sex with another woman? How much freedom is permissible? What about separate vacations? Suppose he wants to go on a fishing or hunting trip with the boys, and you prefer to go with your friends to a beach resort. What if he enjoys going to dances and discos, whereas you prefer an evening at the theater? It may be necessary to write down what rules will govern your relationship. Life is with people, and how we socialize determines much of our happiness or unhappiness. Many marriages have foundered because of different life-styles.

Money. What are the partners' feelings about money? Must the wife ask the husband if she may buy a new dress? Who is to control the checkbook? Shall money be in a joint or separate checking account? What are the financial priorities? Do they have similar attitudes toward saving and spending? Does the wife feel that the family must live in the best neighborhood even though their income does not warrant it? Is one partner a social climber and the other easygoing and disinterested in status? A marriage contract might well offer some guidelines as to how expenses are to be met. It is possible that the husband will expect his wife to work. What if she prefers not to? Should the couple delay having children until they have saved enough for a down payment on a home? The subject of money cannot be avoided.

Relatives. The couple may wish to include in their contract some provision concerning how to deal with in-laws and other relatives. A husband may be unusually close to his mother and a daughter very close to her father. If the in-laws live in the same community, how much time should be spent with family? How do the couple feel about spending holidays and birthdays with one in-law or the other? If one partner has an aged parent, how does the other feel about bringing that person home to live with them? What about the financial support for indigent in-laws? Will this trigger violent arguments and dissension? One young woman declared, "He never liked my parents. When he came to the house he was always cold and distant. He scarcely spoke a civil word to them. After we were married, it was a battle to get him to behave when my folks came over to the house for dinner. Everything was such an effort, where my family was concerned." The husband replied, "Emily's family never felt I was good enough for their daughter. They wanted her to marry a professional man. I earn a living with my hands. They feel I lack status. I just cannot feel comfortable around them. I remember how they inspected my fingernails to see if they were clean. This happened at the wedding. They also look down on my parents because they are blue-collar workers. Emily does not understand. I know she loves her parents, but I also know that I can never be close to them. I guess we just come from different backgrounds. I do the best I can. Frankly, I hope that someday we will move far away from both sets of in-laws. It sure would help our marriage!"

Importance of Work. A marriage contract might deal with how the couple feel about work. Do they each have a driving ambition to get ahead, or are they willing to be satisfied with the simple joys and pleasures of living each day. A couple came to see me to set their wedding date. The bride's father was a hard-driving businessman, and his wife was very socially conscious. A big, fashionable wedding was planned. The betrothed couple were easygoing and low key. The bride's mother exclaimed, "Here we are plannng a big wedding, worrying about all the details, and the kids have not even had their blood test yet, nor have they applied for a license. They always do everything at the last minute. Here it is less than two months before the wedding, and she hasn't yet gone to look for a wedding dress." The couple spoke softly to the parents and tried to calm them down. They were getting married with slim job prospects, but they felt that things would work out somehow. They were not terribly worried about what tomorrow would bring. As struggling young musicians, they felt they could get along. The parents were obviously distressed by the lack of ambition shown by the groom. Yet, from my point of view, the couple seemed to be well suited to each other. Neither placed much stress on material things. They were young, poetic, dreamy souls who had found each other. You could tell that they had a great deal in common. They were not about to make work and a job that important to their marriage.

Children. Central considerations should be how many (if any) children the couple would like to have and their timing. Do they plan to wait to start a family until they both have finished college and are established in their careers? What if the wife becomes pregnant while she is in college? Should she have the baby or seek an abortion? Who is to decide if, for any reason, the husband or wife feel that an abortion is necessary. What about the raising of the children? How shall discipline be handled? To what extent is the husband willing to assist in household chores relating to the rearing of the young? Do they honestly feel they will be good parents, or do they prefer a childless marriage with greater freedom to travel and less financial responsibility? Central to any contractual marriage should be a frank discussion of how the couple really relate to the notion of facing parenthood. A young woman sighs, "I always wanted children, and Len didn't. I thought I could change him. I never faced the fact that he was really serious about not having a family. I have always loved children, and in my heart I hoped to have a house full of them. I was so in love with Len that I felt my love for him would cause him to want what I wanted. Now our marriage is in trouble. I feel he is self-centered and egotistical not to want kids. He says that if we have children, I will neglect him. I wish he would grow up. I'm tired of playing house in a home without a child. We have been married for four years. We have a huge emotional investment in our marriage. But unless he agrees to having a family, we shall soon divorce." They say that love is blind, and in this case it blinded a young woman to the definite ideas of her spouse. She learned too late that her husband really meant it when he said he wanted a childless marriage.

Premarriage Counseling

Another possible aid to preventing divorce is premarriage counseling with a counselor or clergyperson. Some psychiatric and religious institutions sponsor premarriage courses. Few couples are really interested in what should be most vital to them, that is exploring together what they will actually face in marriage to determine if they are capable of handling their future relationship and its problems. Premarriage counseling succeeds best if a couple are required to attend. Some Catholic groups strongly urge couples to have premarriage counseling. Couples I have talked to have said that they were happy they took such instruction. The problem is that most couples do not seek it, and few clergypersons are prepared to devote the time and effort to such assistance.

Communal Living

The commune was popularized in the 1960's as young people sought new ways of expressing themselves. Some saw in the Israeli *kibbutz* a model for communal living in America. Communes take many forms. Originally, most of them were rural and agricultural. More recently, we have seen the formation of city communes, numbering from as few as a handful to as many as twenty or more persons. The commune attracts people who are willing to share a very open life-style. Privacy becomes difficult, and cooperation and sharing become paramount. In some communes one does find dropouts from society. They attract persons who were formerly married and are lonely; within the commune they can find multiple attachments and friendships. For some, this is better than a monogamous relationship with a single person. Communal living attracts only a small percentage of the population; most find it restrictive. Perhaps the Israeli collective has succeeded because it preserves monogamy, while allowing for communal rearing of the children and sharing of most worldly goods.

Staying Together

It is interesting to note that some psychologists now feel that staying married may be a better answer than divorce. Harvard psychologist William Appleton and his wife, Jane, have written a book, *How Not to Split Up,* presenting reasons for people to stay together.

Divorce is very expensive; lawyer's fees can range well over $1,000. The columnist Sylvia Porter has pointed out that a divorced man with two children may lose one-third to one-half of his income in child support and alimony payments. In addition, there are the loneliness and the destruction of your regular daily routine. Divorce involves considerable adjustment of one's life-style. The Appletons say that many people find they cannot concentrate on their work and are discouraged by their new social situation. The Appletons hold that it can take up to four years to adjust to one's new station in life.

The Appletons counsel those considering divorce to look at your marriage honestly to see where you are at fault. Can you blame everything on your spouse? And if your marriage is dull, why not look back to the days when you were single. Maybe you were bored and unhappy then, too.

Some blame their children for a lack of affection between the spouses. The Appletons feel that children can add a wonderful dimension to a marriage; they can enhance, rather than lessen, love. A telling point the Appletons make is, "You would not dine in the same place, wear the same clothes, or be otherwise dull and repetitive with someone you were trying to impress or stimulate. So, why do it with your husband or wife?" A good marriage is not a gift. One cannot just sit back after the wedding ceremony and expect everything to be smooth sailing. Effort must be expended.

At a time when many psychologists favor open expression of thoughts and feelings, the Appletons advise holding one's tongue. Think before you speak. Back off, rather than attack. But if you must disagree, try to make it a negotiating session as you discuss specific problems. A vicious free-for-all may ruin a marriage beyond repair.

Going Slow

Is it wise to rush into divorce? For most people this is not a good idea. We know that divorce American style is not difficult for many to attain, but it is not a matter to be taken lightly. The question of whether or not to break up demands serious thought. As a young adult you will enter into marriage filled with idealism. You will fantasize what your life will be like. If you work hard at it, you have a chance to make your fondest dreams come true!

Thought Questions

1. Do you think that there are any effective alternatives to divorce?
2. Would you like to be part of a trial marriage? What would be good or bad about it?
3. Do you think that a limited contractual marriage could really work?
4. What role should money and the disbursement of funds play in a marriage? Why does money sometimes lead to divorce? Do you believe in joint checking accounts?
5. Why do so many advocate premarriage counseling? Do you think it would help lower the divorce rate? Why or why not?
6. Do you think that communal living will ever attract large numbers of people? Why or why not?

CHAPTER IX

Fantasyland

I have often felt that people project their fantasies when they are in love. A teenager will gush over the latest rock star. A middle-aged man or woman will be thrilled by the sight of a still handsome but aging TV or motion picture personality. The word "fantasy" has become part of our vocabulary. A psychologist might ask a patient, "Why don't you fantasize what you would most like to see in your marriage?" When the question is asked, a number of answers spring quickly to mind.

Continuous Undying Affection

We look at our beloved with the eyes of love. Our fantasy is that the person we adore does truly love us. Often there is jealousy if he or she shows interest in someone else. A person in love becomes overprotective and often over demonstrative. Our expectations of romantic love may exceed our partner's ability to realize them. In the courtship period, we are on our best behavior. We try to live up to the fantasy. We treat our beloved with much more affection than we would ever extend to others in our families. Lovers tend to create their own private world. They see the world through the eyes of love. It is an idealization of one's mate that occurs. Flaws are minimized.

Consideration of My Needs

Our love object is visualized as one who is truly considerate of what we want and need. A young man speaks, "Vivian was always the girl I adored. When we were in high school, I pursued her with the greatest of ardor. When we went to college, I made sure that we attended the same university. Her parents sent her away to school hoping that she would meet someone else, but I was right there. Yet, to be completely honest, we would have to admit that I love her far more than she loves me. Our marriage is in trouble. I feel that I am always giving, and she is always receiving. It is not a good situation. I know that she is not working hard enough at making our marriage succeed. I guess it is my fault for putting her on a pedestal. She just does not care that much about my feelings."

The young man had fantasized about his beloved, surrounded her with a mystic aura. Once he had won her hand, he found he had not won her heart. During the marriage they soon saw flaws in each other. The "me"-centered person is very much in evidence in our society. Some are catered to, not only in childhood, but in adulthood as well. In a good marriage, each should be considerate of the needs of the other. Fantasy may make for romance, but it sometimes distorts reality.

Willingness to Change

A popular fantasy of marrying couples is that the partner will be willing to alter his or her life-style so as to be more in harmony with your way of thinking and acting. You may find that you are creating a false picture. Let us suppose that you picture your beloved to be a sweet, innocent, starry-eyed young woman. In reality she may be very down-to-earth, pragmatic, and blunt in expressing herself. Your fantasy is that beneath that severe exterior is a heart of gold that will change through love. Again, reality is distorted. People often do accommodate to each other in small ways, but drastic change is not to be expected.

A husband comments, "I know this seems silly, Dr. Raab, but it really gets my goat that the only time my wife straightens up the house is when her folks are visiting us or we are having company. Otherwise, the place is a mess. I find that I am always picking up and straightening up after her. She never has time to put things away, yet she can talk on the phone for hours on end to her friends." I asked him if he had talked the problem over with his wife. He replied, "I certainly have shown my anger often enough at the way the place looks. She should have gotten the message by now. We've been married for ten years. She should know what bugs me." I advised him to discuss his feelings with his wife. We often expect our mates to be mind readers. It is best to talk things out—not in anger, but calmly. Pick an appropriate time. Don't bring up touchy subjects when your mate is tired, annoyed, or aggravated.

Off by Ourselves

Another popular fantasy is that marriage will be an escape. We will leave our cares and troubles behind and build a new free life in a far-distant place. Wherever you settle there will be new problems and adjustments. Marriages don't exist somewhere over the rainbow. As soon as we wed, we are engulfed by responsibilities and duties.

For most of us, it is pure fantasy to think that we will build our own private ark that can weather the storms of life. It is probably healthy to have such a fantasy if it is not carried to extremes. The honeymoon is a time when the couple go off by themselves, but it is an artificial situation. Only on vacation do you have others waiting on you and catering to your needs. When you have children, even the vacation means responsibility. You do not stop being a parent for a minute.

Never Growing Old

A popular fantasy is that we will never really age. When we are young, our parents appear to be well along in years. The older we become, the more we realize that life has a termination point. We do live in an age of experiments in cloning, and doctors are able to replace parts of the body as they wear out. Cosmetic surgery can bring back a more youthful appearance. Nevertheless, we do age. The firm muscles of youth turn flabby. The cute little girl in the bikini that you married may discover, after her third child, that she really does not look that great in a bathing suit. The athletic young man develops a paunch. The mirror tells us that we simply do not look at 50 the way we did at 20.

As a young adult, you may long to be older. You may not realize that those who are middle-aged and older are yearning to have their youthful good looks again.

Sociologists and psychologists now speak of the mid-life crisis when the male or female sees the fantasy of youth disappear. If people could grow young together, everything would be fine. Such is not the case. The years take their toll, and suddenly a man or woman takes a good look at his or her mate and finds the other wrinkled and aged. A 50th wedding anniversary is an outstanding milestone, especially if the couple reach that age in good health; but many are touchy about revealing their age.

In the never-never land of our fantasies, we remain eternally youthful, filled with vigor and vitality, always meeting every challenge. Young adults should be aware that being young is not a perpetual state. And you should also know that you and your beloved will change.

We Will Not Repeat the Mistakes of Others

Youth believe that there is a special wisdom involved in being young. Every generation feels that it has new and better answers to the questions of life. It would be marvelous if we could learn from the mistakes of previous generations and not repeat them. Yet the chronicles of humanity reveal a cycle of wars, famine, disease, and destruction. Each generation, so it seems, must find out for itself what is right and what is wrong.

Is it possible not to repeat errors? Probably not. Youth have to learn for themselves, painful as this may seem to their elders. It is good to enter marriage filled with idealism and a determination to make your marriage succeed. Yet the fantasy persists that we can do better than previous generations or better than others of our own generation.

The problem as I see it is not the mistakes that are made but how you deal with them. Two people who live together soon discover that each is an individual unto himself or herself. Mistakes need not be fatal. In a good marriage, mistakes are to be laughed about and not repeated. If you are tolerant of your mate, everything eventually works itself out. There has to be a sense of dedication and purpose. If you have this, no problem is unsolvable.

Life Gets Better and Better

A natural fantasy is that your marriage will improve with the years. In the words of Ben Ezra: "Grow old along with me! The best is yet to be. The last of life, for which the first was made . . . see all, nor be afraid." These lines by Robert Browning express the deepest longing of the human heart. There are marriages that, like fine wine, do improve with age, but reality can play tricks on us. An unexpected illness of a spouse or a child can dim the luster of life. Business reverses can crush the spirit. Social problems may blight a relationship. Things do not always work out according to our plans and dreams.

If life is to get better and better, we must work diligently to make it so. Marriage, like any human undertaking, requires constant attention. It should be a team effort, with the players sharing common goals and working to realize them.

Dreaming

It is not bad to be a dreamer. The biblical Joseph had dreams and was able to make them come true. Most of the high achievers are able to combine natural talent with hard work, so that their dreams of success are reached. Young people are accused of being idealistic, naive, and trusting. Yet it is one of the virtues of the young that they have not been hardened by the lessons taught in the school of hard knocks.

At the same time, do not let go of your dreams. The vision of a better world where people can be happily married is nothing to be ashamed of. Good dreams are the stuff of which reality is formed. There is a time to dream and a time to be pragmatic and realistic. In a good marriage you need both. Shared dreams come true if a couple think along similar lines and develop common priorities of action. Marriages that should work begin to fail, because spouses take each other for granted. The dream will die unless it is tended.

Thought Questions

1. How would you define the word fantasy?
2. Is it really important to have fantasies about the future? Why or why not?
3. Is it realistic to expect love to last forever? Should couples divorce when one falls out of love?
4. Do you think that people ever change? What is the danger in marrying someone with the expectation that you can change him or her?
5. Why does the youth culture sometimes lead to divorce? Does our society place too much emphasis on retaining one's youthfulness?
6. Should you enter marriage with the expectation that life with your spouse will continually get better and better?
7. Must we have realistic expectations when we enter into marriage?
8. Does being a dreamer help or hinder a marriage? Why?

CHAPTER X

Final Thoughts

A religious tradition says that we were put upon this earth to complete God's work of creation. According to this approach, the world is always in a state of becoming, and humans will always face problems. Another philosopher wrote that it is not our role to complete the task, but we must not desist from doing our part. Whatever one's religion or lack of it, it is evident that our world is far from complete. This planet is in a continuous state of change, and all of us humans are changing day by day. Everything we say or do is in some way derived from traditions and people who have preceded us. We do not emerge full-blown into this world. From infancy, we carry with us something of our parents and grandparents. Yet, we can fashion our own ideas in harmony with the modern world we inhabit. The sociology of our experience is grounded in the reality of life as we live it. Someone said, half jokingly, that no one gets out of this world alive.

Pressures

Society generates much pressure upon us. Living as we do in a pleasure-oriented era, the greatest desire of most people is to lead as pain-free and surprise-free a life as possible. Though many say they are stimulated by change, the body resists too violent upheavals. The ideal marriage is one in which pressures can be minimized and bickering kept under control. Beyond that, persons do seek fulfillment through living in harmony with another individual. Yet, there is a great desire not to be suffocated by one's spouse. Much is said about having room to grow. The lock-step marriage of an earlier generation has been replaced by a more easygoing partnership lifestyle that demands respect for all the individuals in the family.

Work

Work is no longer seen by many of the young as the ultimate goal of life. To be happy means that you work at something that gives you pleasure, but you do not sacrifice yourself to the job. In an age of test-tube babies and genetic engineering, we are not as rooted in time, place, and space. Mobility is the hallmark of civilization. We go where the job is and hope that it will be satisfying. If it is not, then we look around and go somewhere else. There is less and less stigma to changing jobs frequently. Life is largely unfinished, as people hunger for new experiences and new thrills. It is no wonder that the institution of marriage has suffered. If people go where the jobs are, the uprooting can be painful and cause strain upon personal relationships. Leaving old surroundings may not be pleasant. In a fast-paced world where life is in constant flux, people often become like objects that are useful and amusing for a while, but in time we discard friends, neighbors, business associates, and spouses.

The Young

If roots are superficial, then the young are affected. Previous generations were shown the way by an older generation that had some sense of purpose and direction. The immigrants who settled America had a good idea of who they were and where they were going. In this promised land they could fashion a newer and better life, and in the process they hoped to hand down values to their children. The immigrants of the early 20th century, however, discovered that they had to learn from their own children, since they could not speak the language or easily master the dress, style, and culture of the emerging American way of life. But with all the stress and upheaval, a clear bond still linked one generation to the next. A child might feel his parents were old-fashioned, but the ideas of the permanency of marriage and the necessity to stay together for the sake of the children were paramount. It is in the past 15 or 20 years that the divorce rate has taken such a giant leap upward, and it is in the second-generation Americans that we see the ever-growing breakdown of the family structure.

How do the young react to the breaking up of the home? It is bound to have its impact as children take sides against one or the other parent. In some cases, they may even feel guilty and think that they were at fault. If a child overhears a father say, "If it weren't for the darn kids you might pay more attention to me," that child is certain to be troubled. Children in our society must wait many years before they are economically independent. When there is divorce, the child wonders if he or she will be able to go to college and to lead a normal life as it used to be. The one-parent family has not yet become the norm, even though such situations are becoming more common. Although spouses are concerned about the welfare of the children, it is not likely that an unhappy home will remain intact just for the sake of the children.

Your Role

If you see that your parents are divorcing, is there anything you can do? Well, you should realize that you are probably not the cause of the split-up, or even if you are the cause, it is not your responsibility. You did not ask to be born. Once you are born, those who brought you into the world have a responsibility to rear, comfort, and protect you. Legally, society must take care of you until you reach the age of 18. If your home is in turmoil, it may be difficult to know what to do. You may find that each parent is pulling at you, seeking your approval and favor. It is difficult to avoid the quicksand of partisanship, especially when the stakes are high. A judge may ask you which parent you wish to live with, and you will have to answer as honestly as you can. As a young adult, there may be little that you can do to bring your parents together. In rare cases your advice may be sought, but usually children are simply told by one or both parents that the marriage is terminating. The reasons you are given may or may not seem valid. If you can, try to proceed with your normal routine. Your parents may go out of their way to try to be nice, so as to maintain a full degree of normality. You can be helpful if you go along with all efforts to keep things on an even keel. Tantrums and recriminations and words of hatred directed at either or both parents will serve no useful purpose. In most instances, both of your parents love you. The problem is with them, not with you. The chances are that both parents have terrible feelings of guilt, whatever the cause of the divorce. They do not need to be reminded of their failings.

If your parents cannot be of comfort, you may wish to seek reassurance from other relatives. You may have a close friend in whom you can confide. It gives some relief to be able to talk to someone about your feelings. If you can approach your clergyperson or your family doctor, there may be helpful insights to be gleaned.

It is vital to realize that you are not alone. Your parents, anguished though they may be, are still there, and others in the family, as well as friends, can assist you during troubling times.

If you are friendly with someone whose parents are splitting up, you can be a source of comfort and aid to them. Don't just say, "Is there anything I can do?" Instead, make a specific suggestion. You might wish to suggest that she sleep over at your home for a weekend or take a trip with you and your family. If you can include your friend in your normal routine, she will know that she is not alone.

Invite her to go to a movie or to the beach with you. See that she is surrounded by your circle of friends. Do not let her withdraw and become depressed. Even if you cannot get your friend to change her mood, the very fact that you are standing by is enormously helpful. Make allowances for the mood your friend is in. If she makes sarcastic remarks or behaves strangely, make allowances. Her very lifestyle is being threatened. You may be one of the few links she has with her normal activities and routine. The worst thing you can do is to exclude her on the theory that maybe it would be better to leave her alone now. Friends are not just for happy times. We need them even more when things are going badly.

What Will Happen to Me?

Divorce can terrify the children. What will become of me if dad leaves. How will I survive if my mother walks out? What will people say? How can I face my friends at school? Can I pretend that everything is all right when I know that things are really scary. Will dad support us, now that he is moving away and mom does not have a job? Will we have to go and live with our grandparents if dad does not give mom any money? Will we still live in our house? Will we be moving away? Will mom get another man to support us? Will she have trouble getting another husband because we are around? If she starts dating, will we like the new man? Could dad ever get a new wife, after being married so long to mom? What can I do in this strange new setting? These and many other thoughts may race through the minds of the children. Their world is no longer the same. The one word—divorce—has wrought a tremendous change.

Why Divorce?

No one has agreed as to why there are divorces. A multitude of reasons have been advanced. In some cases money is the factor. Usually it is because there is too little of it; in some cases too much money is at the root of the problem. A young woman remarked, "Diamonds, furs, fancy clothes, and expensive cars were not what I really wanted. Mark felt that he could not be a success unless he could give me those things. I tried to convince him that money was not important, but he wouldn't listen. He works day and night to accumulate more and more. We seldom see him. He has become a workaholic. I wonder when he will find the time to enjoy the wealth he is accumulating. He is not the Mark I married twenty years ago. He does not even realize that we are on the verge of a divorce. What is worse, he will hardly notice it if I take the kids and leave him. As it is, he is seldom home. If we go, he will probably move into his office and live there. How could a person be so foolish?" There are persons who are enslaved by the almighty dollar.

In other cases, divorce occurs because the husband does not earn enough money. One young woman declared, "How can Al hold his head up when he—a man of 37—is earning so little? I know he could do better, but he is just plain lazy. He is a wonderful husband and father, but that is not enough. There are bills to pay, and he just cannot make enough. Even with me working part-time, we are always deeply in debt. I married him because I loved his casual, affectionate manner. Well, he hasn't changed. He is just too casual. It hurts me to have to juggle the checkbook and evade the creditors. He doesn't seem to mind."

Money is not always the reason for divorce. There can be emotional and psychological factors. People may not be attuned to each other. If both are strong-willed and unwilling to compromise, the marriage is bound to become turbulent when areas of disagreement emerge. Someone remarked that marriage is a condition where two become as one. The question is, which one? If neither can give ground, trouble is ahead.

Then, too, there can be families in which one mate dominates for a number of years. Finally, the passive partner has had enough and decides he or she wants out of the relationship. A good marriage has give-and-take. On some issues the husband dominates, on others, the wife, and on many issues there is a meeting of minds based on discussion and compromise. A wife declares, "I hoped that John would begin to show some strength. When we were first married I warned him, 'John, do not always give in to me. If you do, we will both be miserable.' Well, he is so eager to please me that life has become dull and predictable. I end up thinking for both of us. He does not make a move without first consulting me. He has become totally dependent on me for everything. Instead of loving him for it, I find that I am beginning to hate him."

Not everyone knows for sure why they get married. Initially, there is physical attraction, or perhaps the fear that one is getting older. Pressures may be exerted by the family that a particular boy or girl is a good "catch." Maybe everyone in your crowd is getting engaged, and you can be swept along with the gang. Biology has a lot to do with marriage. After the age of 18 a strong sexual desire asserts itself. A young wife sighs: "I will never really understand why Harold and I got married. I guess I always felt he was the best-looking guy in our crowd, and it looked like he had a good future in business. All the girls were chasing him. When he began courting me, I was really flattered, and when he proposed marriage I said yes—much too quickly. We were engaged after a whirlwind courtship of two months. Before we knew it, our folks were planning a big wedding for us. Then, after we got married, we took a good look at each other. We really are not the same kind of person. Our interests are totally different. Yes, people say we make a handsome couple, but looks are not enough. Not even good sex is enough to make a happy home. We have been to see a lawyer. Lucky for us we have no kids. How easy it is to drift into marriage. How foolish we were!"

Nothing in Common

It becomes difficult to make a marriage function if your interests and enthusiasm are seldom the same. It is good for each spouse to have things that they enjoy doing alone, but it is far better if they have many of the same interests.

This notion may shock the young. Opposites do attract, but they seldom stay together long. If you share the same religion, culture, status, interests, and ideas, your chances of staying married are excellent. Sameness does not make for divorce and need not make for a dull and boring relationship.

If both of you enjoy similar sports and cultural pursuits, this is a definite plus. If you have the same attitude to having a family, this is another big virtue. If you can agree on raising children—as to discipline, schooling, what neighborhood to live in, and the like, you are more likely to be on the road to success.

Even status plays a role. If we are used to a certain life-style, even the most passionate embrace may not compensate for a downward adjustment in our life-style. We are products of our own sociology. Our ideas and values are learned from our environment. If we are brought up one way, it is difficult to change, and if too drastic a change is demanded, we may be crushed.

It goes against the words of poets and romantics, but it is better to marry someone you have known, and possibly grown up with in your own community, than to marry the mysterious stranger who suddenly comes into your life. Mysterious strangers are to be avoided if long-term happiness is your goal.

Falling in Love and Staying in Love

It is one thing to fall in love. It is another thing to stay married. The first is easy. You meet someone, and the adrenalin begins to flow. You find that you are having fun. The initial contact goes well. But give it time. It is best not to rush relationships. Let them mature and ripen at their own pace. Love is a maturing process. Love is part of marriage, and it is expressed in many ways. If you love someone, you will help around the house. If you see your mate is tired, you will start supper and do the dishes. If she looks worn out you will say, "Honey, why don't we eat out tonight?" If she is going grocery-shopping, you volunteer to go along and help. In a thousand ways you can demonstrate that you care. When children arrive, it is best if both spouses pitch in with the additional duties. The father as well as the mother can get up to feed the baby or rock the crib. Love is a complex concept. It is defined as a sense of mutuality growing out of shared respect, as two people seek common goals and assist each other to reach them. No task should be demeaning. If it has to be done, either can perform it.

Listening and Communicating

Some people do not hear each other. It is not that they are deaf. They simply do not concentrate on what the other person is saying. There is an old expression—tuning someone out. It conjures up a picture of a person turning off his hearing aid so he will not have to hear what the other party is saying. Some would rather talk than listen. Often people do not hear because they believe they already know the answer. In marriage we need to be sensitive to the tone of the voice and the expression. The words and facial expression may not match. Part of the success in marriage is learning how to listen and being sensitive to the true feelings of others. A woman declared, "I never could get through to him. He tuned me out. His mind was always a million miles away. At first, I thought he was deaf, but his hearing was fine. He managed to hear what he wanted to hear. The more I screamed, the less he heard. I couldn't reach him. Then I discovered that his secretary in the office was getting to him. Well, we have been to see a lawyer. I bet he will listen carefully to the lawyer when we talk about a divorce settlement."

If we listen we can act with a greater degree of intelligence. The worst thing to do is to shut oneself off from someone else. By ignoring the other person, you may force him to take drastic action.

As a young adult, I am sure you find much to discuss with those you date. It is important that your mate be congenial in conversation. Long silences are not conducive to a long, happy marriage.

Communication is vital. When a couple are communicating, the marriage is working. Few marriages are truly happy if the house is silent, or if only one spouse is always chattering. Communication cannot guarantee that a marriage will last, but it certainly helps if people talk to each other.

It Is Up to You

No one can live your life for you. The ability to make intelligent choices is an individual matter. Some are better able to cope with divorce than are others. There are families that split apart with a minimum of friction. It becomes an individual matter, since no two divorces are exactly alike.

Divorce touches the raw edge of human emotion. It is, for many, a sign of failure. How you cope with divorce will be determined by your attitude toward it. If a divorce is pending in your family, you cannot escape the situation. Running away is no solution. The divorce works itself out day by day. It can be a long process to reach adjustment. If you determine that you will make the best of it and not bring more grief to your parents, you can be vital in initiating and sustaining the healing process. If you are angry and resentful, you will only aggravate an already tense situation.

It takes a degree of maturity to act well when you see your parents acting immaturely. They are too close to the situation to see clearly what is going on, so they may act in an uncharacteristic way that you find distasteful and unpleasant. Be aware that they still love you. It takes time to "work through" the trauma of divorce. Even friendly divorces sap the strength and vitality of the family.

A Final Word

A young woman speaks, "We held our marriage together for 14 years for the sake of the children. We have two lovely young daughters. Every time we spoke of divorce, the children pleaded with us not to. We felt their world would be destroyed. Now my husband has moved out, and the world did not fall apart. The children are adjusting, even though they are not thrilled by the arrangement. My ex-husband and I have discovered that kids are much tougher and more resilient than we give them credit for being. Things are working out. My ex and I are both starting to date others. We know it will not be easy, but it is better now, with no more fights and bitter arguments. We should have parted years ago. Our value systems are not the same. We each have discovered people we can be comfortable with and not be hassled. There are other people in the world who have needs more like ours."

More and more, couples are concluding that if love is gone and nothing is left except bitterness, then—painful though it be—divorce is better than an unhappy marriage. When partners cannot communicate and counseling has failed, the last step becomes divorce.

Children and parents are survivors. I believe that most have untapped resources of strength in the most difficult times. You, as a young adult, should be able to muster the fortitude to withstand the shock of divorce if it comes to your own family. And you may be able to agree with the couples who honestly believe that divorce is better than a failed marriage.

There is life beyond divorce. For most Americans, there is the strongest of possibilities that they will remarry. The majority of divorced persons do find a new mate, and these second marriages have an excellent chance of success. Love and marriage are quite in step with today's life-style. We seek affection, and there is a good chance we will find it.

As Heine wrote:

> To love and be loved, this
> On earth is the highest bliss.

Thought Questions

1. Why does the work ethic get in the way of marital happiness? Can a workaholic make a good husband or wife?
2. To what extent should the life-style of our parents influence the way we will live once we are married?
3. Why do some fall in love and make a go of marriage whereas others fail?
4. What do we mean when we say communication is vital to a good relationship? Can marriages survive when communication ceases? Why or why not?
5. How much control do we have over our lives?
6. What can a person do to comfort a friend whose parents are getting a divorce?

Bibliography

Appleton, William and Jane. *How Not to Split Up*. New York: Doubleday, 1978.

C.B.S. News Almanac. Maplewood, N.J.: Hammond Almanac, Inc.

Collier's Encyclopedia, Vol. 8. New York: Macmillan, 1978.

Encyclopedia Americana, Vol. 9. New York: Americana Corporation, 1973.

Fleischmann, Karl. "Marriage by Contract: Defining the Terms of Relationship." *Family Law Quarterly*, Vol. 8, No. 1, Spring 1974. American Bar Association.

Fromm, Eric. *The Art of Loving*. New York: Harper, 1956.

Horton, Paul B., and Hunt, Chester L. *Sociology*. New York: Knopf, 1975.

Krantzler, Mel. *Creative Divorce*. New York: M. Evans and Company, 1974.

Leslie, Gerald R. *The Family in Social Context*. New York: Oxford University Press, 1976.

Light, Donald, Jr., and Keller, Suzanne. *Sociology*. New York: Knopf, 1975.

O'Neill, Nena and George. *Open Marriage*. New York: M. Evans, 1972.

Sheehy, Gail. *Passages*. New York: E. P. Dutton, 1976.